I0749671

Believers in Love

Alan Clay

Artmedia Publishing
www.artmedia.com.au
epublish@artmedia.com.au

Believers in Love
First Edition, September 2001
ISBN: 0957884400

Typeset in Bookman Old Style
Printed in America and England by Lightning Source.

Giving Meaning

Sarah sat at the side of the road, with what looked like the contents of her pockets spread out on a towel before her.

"What are you doing?" her father asked.

"I'm fishing for trout," the girl told him.

The father looked amused, but said nothing, and determined to watch how the game proceeded. Soon a passer-by stopped, and asked Sarah the same question.

"I'm writing a book." she responded.

Each person who stopped to ask, and the father counted fifteen in about ten minutes, was given a different answer.

"How many trout have you caught?" he finally asked.

"About fifteen in the last ten minutes," the girl answered.

Sax

My laughing Buddha sat looking peacefully out from the mandala of raked sand beneath the bonsai on the table, while beside it, from the front page of yesterday's paper, stared the forlorn face of a child.

I felt exhausted and confused. I followed the Buddha's gaze out, between my brightly patterned curtains, to the wash of morning traffic in Taylor Square. A large Aboriginal woman wandered out onto the road, drinking from a bottle hidden in a brown paper bag and shouting obscenities to an imaginary partner. A truck blared its horn as it had to swerve to avoid her, and she abused it, in turn.

My eye fell back on the bonsai. This was the third I had made. The peacefulness of the raked sand, safely enclosed by the rim of the bowl, seemed insignificant however, beside the chaotic reality outside.

I looked again at my comfortable living room, and I suddenly saw how the confines of my world also presented just an artificial barrier between me, and the vast whirl of experience, from which I was actually hiding.

I felt a rush of energy in my spine at this realization, and small beads of sweat broke out on my brow. For a moment, I felt like I was standing on the edge of a cliff, and then a laugh of relief bubbled up through my exhaustion and I got up, as if surrendering to the inevitable.

I discovered my saxophone hanging on a coat-peg by the door, and I swung it over my shoulder. I was breathing hard as I pounded down the stairs, but as I stepped out from the apartment building, I suddenly felt free, and I savored the warmth of the early spring sunshine.

An empty table stood outside my favorite cafe, but it felt good to let my body walk, and so I simply kept moving. I had no idea where I was going, and the wonderful openness of this feeling filled my chest with excitement.

I found a pavement artist on the corner of Crown Street, and I was arrested by the colors of her work. She was kneeling on a cushion, working the chalk confidently onto the black bitumen, and the texture of the colored chalk on the pitted surface reminded me of my sand designs.

She sat back on her haunches and surveyed her creation. She was a colorful sight herself, red leather sneakers, glittery knee-high socks, fishnet garters, shiny yellow hot pants and a leopard skin halter top.

"Excellent," I commended her.

She looked up. "You look like you need a good night's sleep," she said with disarming familiarity.

I grinned. I felt embarrassed. "I haven't been able to for the past few nights," I confessed. I fished a coin out of my pocket and dropped it in her hat.

"You should do yoga," she suggested brightly, and, as if to demonstrate, she adjusted her feet so they splayed out beside her hips and sat between them. She looked like a little kid in that posture.

"It's okay, I'm off to seek my fortune," I responded, surprising myself with my own flippancy.

Her eyes danced lightly for a moment, and she pulled a card out of her pocket and gave it to me. On one side was her name, Zoe, in letters as large as the card itself, and on the other, it read: 'You are invited to the opening of an exhibition at Artspace in Woolloomooloo.' I checked the date and discovered it was next Friday.

"Thanks," I told her. "I'll try and make it."

She smiled, and bowed her head. It felt like the relationship had become almost too intimate for comfort, and I was about to walk off, when she noticed my sax. "You play?" she asked.

I nodded.

She motioned to the doorstep of the bank behind her, which was not yet open. "Play for a while," she suggested. "We'll split the hat."

There seemed no reason not to take up the suggestion, so I sat down and allowed the notes of my instrument to flow out over her colors, and mingle with the feet of the passers by.

Zoe

Zoe dropped her street-bag inside the door. It had been a good morning, and the weight of the coins in the hat thudded, as the bag hit the floor. She liked Sax, she hoped they would see more of one another.

Minx got up from the sheepskin by the fireplace and stretched. His little back arched and his fur stood on end. Then his body relaxed, and he padded over to rub against her leg. She bent down and scratched behind his ears and he started purring. The noise seemed unnaturally loud for such a little kitten.

"It's all so simple for you, isn't it?" she told him, picking him up and cradling him in her arms. "Just lying in the sun and eating." He started kneading her with his paws and nuzzling into her chest with his head, and the purring got louder.

She carried him across the open studio to her

workbench, and placed him on it. He curled up, happy to be right in the middle of whatever she was doing. A satisfying stack of paintings stood beside the bench, ready to go to the exhibition. She had already wrapped some in newspaper, and these looked like giant mystery packages, while others were stacked beside them, a jumble of colors and tantalizing glimpses.

One untouched canvas sat on the bench. She picked it up, placed it on the easel, and felt the pull of desire to play with it. She wanted to do something special with this one, but wasn't certain what. The bristles of her favorite brush were hard, and she softened them in her hand as she considered the white surface.

Her eye caught her sketchbook on the bench, and she leafed through the sketches from last weekend's yoga workshop. There were some good ones. She felt relieved, she was paying for the workshops with the artwork for a new poster.

Her eye was drawn back to the canvas, but she still found no inspiration in the blank surface. There was a weird sound and she felt a sensation like a presence in the room. A shiver ran down her back, and her hand sought the texture of a gemstone in her pocket, until the feeling passed.

Then the phone rang. The noise startled her and she gasped. Minx opened one eye, went to stretch, and relaxed back into sleep. Acting on intuition, she let the machine take the call. "Hi Zoe, it's Jess... I'm sorry for what happened last week... It's over between me and Sam... and I know you'll find it hard to trust me now, but..." She quickly crossed to the machine, turned the volume down, and stood watching it take the rest of the message in deliberate silence. She pushed the delete button and the counter re-set to zero.

She walked back to Minx. Her emotions were seething, and she rested her elbows on the bench and let her head fall into her hands. He nuzzled against her. He was such a furry little ball that her heart opened and she felt tears in her eyes. He started purring loudly.

She turned back to the easel and realized she was putting off the moment when she would have to commit herself to the canvas. Its emptiness stared provocatively back at her.

Some bills were hanging from a bulldog clip above her workbench. These debts worried her, but she knew it was always like this as she approached an exhibition. When she had sold a few paintings, she would be okay. Anyway, that's why she was going out in the street, she told herself.

She always felt so assured working in the street, when people were watching her, and yet she sometimes felt like a bag of insecurities when she was by herself. She almost needed an audience to keep her focused, she realized, and she tried to imagine a few people wandering around the studio.

She picked up the old tray that she was using as a pallet, squeezed some paint onto a clear area, mixed it with her brush, and made a few quick strokes on the canvas.

She stood back to view the change. The surface already had a texture, which suggested images. She made a few more strokes. There seemed to be an animal there, or a landscape with lots of people, or a face staring out at her. She mixed some shades and allowed nuances to grow.

Her imagination became fired up, and she saw herself hanging her pictures in the gallery next week. She had enjoyed this fantasy several times a day recently: she watched herself unwrap each one carefully, and choose exactly the right spot to display it, before Minx leapt off the bench and rubbed about her legs.

Back in the reality of the studio, the almost empty canvas stared at her, and her euphoria slowly subsided and she began to feel frustrated that she was unable to focus on something that was so important.

She really had no skill at this, she told herself, and she considered doing some yoga instead. At least then she would experience something real, and feel satisfied. It always felt like she was groping in her imagination so much, that she valued the realness of the physical world.

She turned back to the canvas one last time, took some black paint and placed another few quick strokes across it, as if to cross it out, then stood back and looked at it. The energy and strength of these last strokes however had enlivened the canvas again, which had begun quietly to sing.

What she liked about art was that you had to put aside your conscious attitudes both to do it, and also to view it, and with this realization she dissolved into the work for a few satisfying hours.

Allowing Change

I met Sarah after school. She was coming up to her eighth birthday. Her shirt was hanging out, and one knee looked grazed, but she was still as cute as a flower.

"Hi dad!" she greeted me brightly. "Guess what we did today."

I kissed her on the forehead. "I don't know," I admitted.

"We played tennis, in sport."

I nodded. She liked games. "I thought we might play a game this weekend."

"What sort of game?" she skipped on the spot.

"A game where we don't do anything that we normally do."

Her eyes brightened, and we were about to walk off down Crown Street, when she put out her arm and stopped me. "We always go this way," she reminded me.

I smiled, and we turned and walked in the other direction. She took my hand. I had a wonderful sense of lightness and enjoyed the warm feelings between us.

“You happier now?” she asked.

I nodded and realized how much my recent mood must have affected her. “It’s the game,” I explained.

She nodded. "Why have you got your sax?"

"I did some busking in Oxford Street this morning."

Her eyes grew round. "You!"

I nodded. My pocket was still full of coins from my split of the hat, and I jangled them to validate my claim. I felt the stiff card of the invite to Zoe's exhibition, and my fingers caressed the texture.

Sarah fell silent, and I imagined she was considering the wider implications of our game, as we approached the corner of Oxford Street. "Does that mean we can't go home tonight?" she asked, and I thought that I heard a quiver in her voice. I shrugged and yet I felt the weight of responsible society judging my reckless actions, and I stole a glance at her. "Maybe we could stay in a hotel then,” she suggested, wide eyed.

I breathed a sigh of relief. "That's a good idea," I

agreed.

We stopped on the corner, wondering about our next move, and watching the parade of people moving up and down the street. There was a real mixture, from the gay and lesbian couples to the tidy tourists and the ragged street people.

Sarah suddenly stiffened. "What about Firefly?"

“What about her?” I responded.

“She won’t know where we are!” Little tears appeared in the corner of her eyes.

"She's an angel," I reminded her, "she always knows where you are."

She nodded, not quite convinced, and she looked around to try and spot her friend. It was a hot afternoon, and the thought of the beach beckoned me. "Let's go to Bondi," I suggested distracting her.

"We often go to Bondi," she said, but her eyes lit up again.

"But we've never stayed there."

"Can you?"

I nodded. "I think so."

The sweep of the swell rolling onto the sand,

foaming white and fresh, was a welcome relief, as the bus made its way down the last hill to the beach.

We got off outside the Swiss Grand Hotel, and Sarah stood staring at the automatic doors, which were sliding open and closed as people came and went.

"We can stay here," she suggested brightly.

I nodded hesitantly, it probably wasn't the cheapest option. My practical self quickly kicked back in, and wondered how we were going to pay for it. “It would probably be better to get something a little cheaper,” I tried to persuade her, but the excitement in her eyes was hard to resist, and I allowed her to drag me through the door.

The odor of organized comfort assailed us inside. Sarah was very impressed, I could tell, by the way she tried to act normal. I matched her casual style and we booked a room at the reception. I presented my credit card. As far as I knew it was already slightly over its limit, but it would probably work.

As I waited for it to clear however, I found my insecurity playing in my imagination, and from this perspective our game began to feel less like a heroic adventure and more like another way of avoiding my life. Was I simply running away again?

Our room had a balcony over looking Campbell Parade, out onto the beach, and when we opened the doors it seemed like the ocean lapped right up to our window. Sarah bounced on the bed, pronounced it good, and then checked the towels and soap packets in the bathroom. Everything was as it should be.

I stretched out on the bed and felt the exhaustion from several restless nights crawl over me. It felt very comfortable, and after all of the struggle, sleep seemed finally a breath away.

Sarah stood by my head and teased at my hair with her fingers. "Let's go play in the sand," she suggested. "It's too early to go to bed." I grunted. The smell of salt in the air from the open doors was indeed invigorating, but the bed was also very comfortable. "We can make a sand castle," she encouraged me.

I smiled. As a child I had spent many happy hours on the beach, molding the sand into monuments against the elements, fortresses which took hours to create, and were blown or washed away within a day. Working with the elements in that way, with the vastness of the sea about me, I remembered my feeling of the awe of life.

I nodded. "Okay." It took all of my will to energize my body, but as I dragged myself up from the comfortable embrace of the bed, I realized how good it was to feel the physical desire to sleep again.

Sarah

The moon was shining through the curtains, across my bed and onto dad's pillow. He rolled over and made some snorting noises in his sleep. I was too excited to sleep and besides, every time Firefly rolled over, her wings kept poking into me.

"I'm glad you found us," I whispered. She made no reply, she never talked, but we shared a warm moment. "You'll never guess what happened this afternoon on the beach," I told her. Her wings glowed white in the moonlight. I could tell she was interested. "Dad and I were working on this sand-castle for hours, until it stood as high as my middle. It was a masterpiece, cause it had all the spires and turrets and walls, and the beach was crowded, and people were stopping to watch."

Dad snorted and rolled over in his sleep.

I lowered my voice. "That was when I saw this guy

in the suit watching us!" I gave her time to appreciate the significance of this. "He was really watching, like maybe he was a spy or something!" For a moment I thought she had gone to sleep, but I realized she was just pretending, and I let the suspense hang until she opened one eye. The sound of the waves came through the open balcony doors. "Of course I got a stick and drew a circle in the sand around the castle," I explained, "which, you know, protects you from any problems."

Dad rolled over again and mumbled something.

I lowered my voice to a whisper. "Anyway, it worked, because it turns out that the guy runs a festival in Auckland, and he wants dad and me to build a sand-sculpture there!" She smiled. I could tell she didn't believe me. "Really!" I assured her. "Truly! And mum lives in Auckland, and we've been promising her a visit for ages." I could tell that she thought it was another one of my stories.

Dad rolled over again.

"Aren't we flying to Auckland in the morning?" I called out, desperate to verify my story.

He grunted. "What?"

"We're flying to Auckland, aren't we?"

"Yes, darling." He rolled over. "But we've got to get some sleep, if we're going to go."

I looked at Firefly. "See!" I whispered.

"You need to settle down darling," dad told me. "Tell Firefly to go to sleep."

Firefly snuggled back under the blankets, even though she knew that dad couldn't see her.

"Goodnight Dad," I called.

"Goodnight," he mumbled already half way back into sleep.

Understanding

When Sax was overseas he felt disorientated and he went to a tourist office for advice.

"My daughter and I are just in town for a few days," he said, "can you advise us what to do?"

The person behind the desk gave him a map of the town and a range of promotional material. "I'm sure you'll find what you need in there," she said.

Sax gazed uncertainly at the material. He had been hoping for specific advice. "Is this all I need to understand the city?" he asked.

She looked at him. "That's what I have," she told him. "As to your understanding..." She considered for a moment, then shrugged. "I'll have to leave that to you."

Adam

Sax and his daughter pulled up in a taxi as the truck was dropping the load of sand in Aotea Square. Adam shook their hands warmly.

"We had fruit salad for breakfast on the plane," Sarah informed him.

"Is that what it is?" he asked, pretending to brush something off her shirt. She looked down, and he brought his finger up to flick the tip of her nose instead. She was caught by surprise, then grinned and poked out her tongue.

A breath of wind funneled through the square, whipping up some sand from the pile. "We'll need a hose, to dampen this, and stop it moving," Sax observed.

He looked like years of dabbling in encounter groups, or perhaps playing in a pub band, or something similar, had mellowed his view of life. Not many people would get on a plane at a moments notice, like he had, and Adam felt that they might have a lot in common, if they could somehow bridge the lack of any familiar ground between them.

"This is for us?" Sarah exclaimed, looking at the sand.

"Any problems?" Adam asked her.

She blew air out through her lips as she looked around the empty square, then back to the sand. Adam followed her gaze. The square was bounded by three centuries of architecture. The old nineteenth century sandstone Town Hall stood opposite the Aotea Centre, a concrete arts-palace, designed in the mid twentieth century and built thirty years later when it was already out of date, and between them the new glass and steel Planet Hollywood and Imax Cinema multiplex.

He sighed. He had to admit that the small pile of sand looked slightly ridiculous in the middle of the empty concrete space, however in his mind's eye he saw the inflatables for the kids, the musicians on the mobile stage and the place filled with people, and he nodded with satisfaction. It would look good, he decided.

"I guess it's not what I thought," she finally admitted. "It doesn't look the same when it's not on the beach."

They laughed.

"Maybe we'll have to make something different here," Sax said

"Not a castle?" Sarah asked.

Sax looked at Adam.

Adam shrugged. "It's up to you."

He left them to it, and didn't see them again till lunch time. The festival was providing meals for staff under the old town hall, but this was the first day, and Adam found it hard to find a seat, as he negotiated the rows of tables with his lunch tray. He finally discovered an empty chair at the table with Sax and Sarah.

"How's it going?" he asked.

"Better," Sarah said, "now that we've started."

Sax smiled. "She gets negative about things when she's nervous," he explained.

"I do not!" Sarah told him. "Parents are so stupid," she sought Adam's support.

He smiled and took a sip of his soup, but it was stil

too hot to eat. He pushed the tray to one side. "Do you want to see some magic?" he asked her.

She nodded eagerly, her eyes widening. "I'll bet I know how it's done," she said, in a very worldly-wise manner.

He smiled. "We'll see." He took out a pack of cards, and shuffled them. "Take a card," he told her. She waited a long time, as he fanned the pack back and forth in his fingers, but finally she took one. "Show it to your dad," he told her. Sax was looking on with a proud parental look. She placed it back and Adam shuffled, then spread four cards face down on the table. "Point to any two cards," he told her. She chose two, one of which he knew was hers, and he removed the other two cards. "I'm getting you to do the magic," he told her. "Point to one of the two remaining cards." She chose the one that wasn't hers, and he removed it. "What was your card?" he asked.

"Queen of diamonds."

"Turn that one over," he told her, and sure enough, it was the right card. Her eyes widened, and he could see her mind racing for explanations. Her face shone with the effort. She looked at her dad, who shrugged.

Each time the sleight of hand worked, there was a moment of real magic, which Adam loved. In that moment when no explanation can be found for what has occurred, the door to the magic realm opens for each person. Suddenly the world isn't a limited and known quantity, and in that moment, anything becomes possible.

His assistant Barbara was on the phone when he got back up to the office.

"He's just walked in, Councilor," she said. "I'll pass you over." She made a throat cutting gesture with her finger as she passed him the phone. Her eyes were wide.

"Hi, Adam here, Auckland Festival," he introduced himself.

"Are you the person responsible for putting that pile of sand in the square?"

"Yes sir, I am. To whom am I talking?"

"Councilor Thomas..." There was a long pause. Councilor Thomas was notorious for grabbing high profile issues and worrying them to death for his own political purposes, and Adam didn't know quite how to respond. "I wish to complain of the waste of public money involved in this sand exercise," the Councilor continued.

"It's actually very cost effective," Adam assured him, kicking himself for his impulsive decision to include it in the festival. "It's fully funded through the sponsorship and entertainment budgets."

"That's not the point!" Thomas exploded, and Adam held the phone away from his ear. "That's not entertainment!" The Councilors voice sounded like the buzzing of a mosquito from this distance. "We don't pay you to waste our money on that!"

Adam tried to detach himself from his desire to defend the idea, because he sensed it would only make matters worse, however he thought he would try one more thing. "Perhaps you would call it art?" he ventured to suggest.

"No, I would not call it art!" Councilor Thomas's breath was heavy and labored with the struggle to express concepts which he otherwise rarely entertained. "Art has craft and majesty, it's not a pile of sand in the square!" He slammed the phone down.

"We all have different views of art," Adam said into the dead phone. "That's what makes it art."

Barbara's lips were pressed tightly into an 'I could have told you so' line, and she had a glint in her eye which told him that although she knew that he had a history of success with weird ideas, she thought he had gone too far this time.

"The Festival Gala is on Monday night," she reminded him. "The Mayor and Councilors are all expected to attend."

He nodded. "I know."

"You better go and meditate on it," she said dryly.

He nodded.

"Hold my calls," he told her as he left.

It took him ages to still his mind and allow the sensations in his body. The drama kept coming up into his attention and he let it go each time, until he finally felt totally at ease with being right where he was, and allowing each breath.

When he returned to the office it was clear to him that Councilor Thomas would not let the matter rest, and inevitably it would be all over the media, so he determined to take the initiative and he phoned the television news himself.

That done, he released the world to go its course , as of course it would anyway, in the best possible way.

What We Want To See

A man and his partner had an argument.

"I don't think we can live together," the man said.

"Why is that?" the partner demanded.

"Because you always sleep on the right side of the bed," the man replied. "It we had an equal partnership, you'd share it with me."

"But I sleep on the right, because the morning sun comes in the window on that side, and I know you wake up easily."

"Exactly," the man responded. "You would deny me my share of the sun in the morning, and for this reason I think we cannot live together."

Finding My Feet

I slept in for the first time in recent memory, and by the time I got up, I had missed the hotel breakfast, so I showered and headed straight down to the square. It was already hot, and the gray paving stones were absorbing the sunshine with no shade for relief.

I felt light-headed and, for a moment, I couldn't really believe that I was here doing this. Sarah had spent the night at her mother's place and without her stabilizing influence, it might all be a dream. I connected up the hose, and gave the sand a light shower.

A few people had stopped to watch by the time she arrived. She came running up, all breathless and excited, a newspaper under one arm, looking very much the mature young lady. "Sorry I'm late, but Mum had to go up to the shops, on the way."

My heart fell, and I looked about, expecting to see

her mother coming striding up behind her, but she was nowhere in sight.

"She couldn't find a park, so she dropped me off," Sarah explained. "She said, 'congratulations on getting successful'."

It was her highest praise, I knew, but I looked at Sarah, uncomprehending.

"The hotel and the airplane," she told me, as if I was stupid. "The festival." I laughed. I'd always wanted to be successful with my music, and had no luck whatsoever, and here I was successful with something totally unimportant. There must be a lesson there, but I wasn't quite certain what it was.

"But she said the paper didn't look so good?" Sarah had a quizzical look on her face as she tried to decipher the mystery of the world. "Did you see it?"

I shook my head and she handed it to me. On the front page, there was a wide picture of the square, in which the mound of sand looked small and insignificant, with just a few people wandering past, and above it ran the headline; *'Is this the festival we deserve?'*

My heart stopped.

'The new Auckland Festival got off to a disappointing start yesterday, with controversy about the costs involved in a sand sculpture project in Aotea Square. There were also questions as to why we had to bring an Australian over to create the sculpture, and why he had to bring his daughter with him, all at rate-payers expense.' I skipped through to the end. Most of it thankfully wasn't about us. *"It's obvious why Auckland can't get a proper festival off the ground," Councilor Thomas told the Herald, "we just don't employ the right people to run the things!"*

Sarah was looking at me.

I shrugged, at a loss to know how to explain i t. "You want an airplane ride, a hotel, and recognition?" I teased her. She nodded, still waiting for the explanation. "Some people are threatened by new things," I tried, "and they want to say it's wrong."

"Maybe we should have done a castle after all."

I laughed. We had decided on a mountain, which rose out of the flat pavement with houses and beaches nestled into the lower flanks. "Why don't you do a castle on the top?" I suggested.

Her eyes lit up. This was the answer, and she set

about it straight away.

By early afternoon the sun was really hot, and we had to keep spraying water onto the sand to keep it firm, and then sprinkling dry sand on top, to stop it evaporating.

The heat wasn't daunting the skate-boarders however, who were using the concrete steps and the ramps down into the square like a dance floor on which to show off their steps. They were all boys, and, when I looked closely, I discovered groups of girls sitting on seats in the shade of the trees, which stood around the edge of the square. They were chatting and displaying their halter tops and bare limbs.

"Mum thought maybe I could spend a few days with her, before going back," Sarah announced.

"You can stay with her now," I told her. “That’s partly why we’re here.”

"I don't want to." She shook her head. "I want to stay in the hotel." She stopped her work on the castle wall, and looked at me. "How was breakfast?" The porter had built up her expectations about it, when we arrived.

"I missed it," I confessed. "I slept in."

Her mouth dropped open. "You what?"

I grinned and shrugged. We worked in silence for some time, and I thought about the travel arrangements. "Okay," I agreed. "I fly back on Thursday, but you can stay over the weekend, and come back on Sunday. I'll get the tickets rebooked."

She nodded, satisfied. "Why don't you come back on Sunday too?"

"Where would I stay?"

"With me and mum."

She was still holding on to that dream. "I've got something to do in Sydney on Friday," I told her.

She nodded reluctantly. "Have you told the school that I'm away this week?"

I shook my head. "I'll phone them tomorrow."

She looked at me with a look that warned me that I was on notice to keep it together, and I nodded my acceptance of this responsibility.

Sometimes, when I am doing something creative, I can just shut out the rest of the world, and that ability allowed people to come close today and stand watching for ages, without disturbing my concentration, or me disturbing theirs.

Sarah couldn't concentrate on any one thing for long however, so she was always stopping and, seeing this, people would ask her questions.

"We won a sand sculpture competition in Sydney last year," she explained to one businessman.

"That's how success works," he said, tussling her hair. "You win the competition and then a festival invites you to do it some more. Before you know it, you're famous."

Sarah knew that it hadn't worked quite like that, but I watched her decide to leave him with his assumptions. She loved having all the answers, and so this role suited her. I noticed that our story changed slightly as she told it to different people.

Towards the end of the day Adam walked up, together with a lady.

"Any more vicious Councilors on the attack today?" I inquired, as innocently as I could.

He grinned. "All clear so far."

"The paper didn't look so good this morning," I sympathized.

"I think they want us to spend more money on advertising."

"Does it work like that?"

"Not officially." He shrugged. "But I hope the television will come and talk to you tomorrow, and maybe they'll be a bit more positive."

I felt my throat gag at the thought of cameras, but I nodded agreement. I don't know why I trusted him, but I did. For all his card tricks, he did have a bit of the magician about him.

"Television, television..." Sarah chanted as she danced from one leg to the other.

Adam turned to introduce the woman beside him. "This is Trish, the administrator of the Adelaide Fringe, she's here for a few days to learn from our mistakes."

Sarah cuddled against my leg and looked up at the woman. She was impressed. I ran my fingers through her hair.

"I think you're going to be a huge success," she assured us. "I'm going to keep my eye on you."

Steep Yourself In Life

"Why have you achieved nothing great with your life?" one man asked another, when they were both in middle age.

"I spent the first part of my life unsure what to do," the second responded, "and so I was forced to steep myself in life, year after year, in an effort to come to some grasp of the experience."

"I know," the first told him. "I watched you do it... And after all that?"

"After that..." the second mused. "I realize that everything is perfect, just as it is, that nothing great is required, and there is therefore no need to do anything beyond steeping myself in life, so I am simply continuing that process."

Magical Realm

Dad had been trying to wake me for ages. "If we don't get down to breakfast straight away," he finally said, "we won't get any food."

I looked at him out of one eye. I was snuggled deep under the covers with Firefly's warm body beside me, and I didn't want to move. "Breakfast stops at ten," he warned me, as he made for the door. "I'll see you down there, if you make it."

"Okay," I grumbled.

As soon as the door closed I jumped out of bed and discovered it was raining. A big gray cloud hung over the city, and the drops of water on the window changed the shapes of the buildings outside so they looked like something out of a bad fairy tale.

It made me want to go back to bed, but the thought of breakfast was too hard to resist, and I discovered my clothes on the floor and quickly pulled them on. I could feel my hairbrush in my pocket.

The hotel was massive and the lift was full of mirrors and lights. Firefly and I went up and down a few times just to get the feel of it. Then we followed the "Breakfast Room' signs down a long corridor, and when we finally found the serving table, it was laid with so many plates of food that we didn't know where to start.

There was cheese and ham, and eggs, and cereal, and yogurt, and fruit, with different sorts of bread and pastries, and all sorts of things like special packets of jam and butter. I was terrible at making these sorts of decisions and Firefly was no help, but I took one of the pastries with yellow custard stuff, and a cake, and an egg sandwich, and then filled another plate with fruit. Then we set off to find dad.

The nectarine almost rolled off as I carried it, and it took all my concentration to reach the table without a major catastrophe. The carpet had a checkered pattern, and I discovered that if I stuck to the white squares, it rolled a lot less, so I did that.

"I didn't think you'd want to miss it," he said, as I

sat down.

I shook my head. This was an experience of a lifetime. I put the plate of fruit in front of me and the cakes in front of the next seat.

"Firefly's got a sweet tooth this morning," he observed.

"I'll probably have to help her eat them," I admitted.

"I thought as much," he said.

The room was full, and I realized there was tables of artists and others with normal hotel guests. "You can tell the difference," I whispered to Firefly, "because the guests are the couples and families, while the artis ts are those big groups, who are showing off." I nibbled a little of her custard pastry, it was sweet and gooey.

"So, how do you like our game so far?" he asked.

"Cool!" I grinned, but I did have a nagging thought. "Did you phone the school yet?"

He shook his head. "I'll give them a call today."

"Cool!" I repeated, but inside I felt a little guilty. Was it right to treat these things so lightly, I wondered.

Adam came past as we finished eating. "It's not so good with the weather," he said. “I didn't think of that.”

Dad shrugged. "I like it." The weather was a mysterious thing, not fully understandable. The custard pastry however, was very sweet, and it took all my concentration to devour it.

"I mean for the sculpture," Adam said.

Dad nodded. "To me it feels strange to come back to it the next day, and it's still there, just as I left it."

Adam had to think about that. "Not destroyed by the tides, you mean?"

Dad nodded.

Adam looked at him with new respect. "I just hope the media don't have a ball with it," he said, but I couldn't work out what he meant.

"Do a magic trick," I told him, to change the subject, but he just stroked my hair.

"We'll get straight into it as soon as it clears," dad suggested.

Adam nodded "It should clear in an hour or so." He looked down at me. I willed him to do some magic and he crouched down, and pulled a coin out of his pocket. I grinned. He waved it in front of me. "I've got two dollars here," he told me.

"You're rich," I told him. "Can I have it?"

"If you can find it," he said, taking it over into the other hand, with a quick movement, then blowing on it, and when he opened his hand, it had disappeared, right under my nose. This guy was someone special.

"See," I whispered to Firefly. "Didn't I tell you he was something like a spy?"

Then I caught Adam looking at dad.

"Allow me to introduce Sarah's friend, Firefly." Dad motioned to the seat beside me.

Some adults don't get it, like they just don't see Firefly, but Adam thankfully wasn't one of those.

"Delighted," he said. "I'm Adam."

By the time we finished breakfast, the rain had almost cleared. It was still drizzling a little however, and so we waited outside the hotel under the covered balcony. I felt my hair brush in my pocket and I took it out and started brushing my hair. There were knots in it and the brush kept getting caught. I grunted a few times to get dad's attention, and finally he took it and did the rest for me.

“If Adam was really a magician,” I wondered aloud,

“why didn't he just magic away the rain?” Dad grunted and brushed harder to clear some tangles. “I bet I can do it,” I told him. I tapped the ground four times with my right foot, and made a circular movement with my left hand, and by the time he had finished my hair, the drizzle had cleared.

“See.” I grinned.

He smiled. “Remember, you’ve got angels on your side.”

“Just one!”

He took my hand, and we picked our way amongst the puddles around the corner to the square. The sculpture looked forlorn in the middle of the empty wet space. When we got close, we saw that the water had flattened out most of the detail of our work, collapsed my castle almost completely and washed dad's beautiful cliffs out onto the concrete.

"Shit!" I said, when I saw it.

"Don't say that," he told me. He took a broom and started sweeping up the sand that had been washed out onto the concrete.

"All that work!" I protested.

"We're here each day anyway," he said. "This way it can change."

I shrugged and we set about repairing it. The basic structure was still fine and, when I got into it, I found that the soaking from the rain had actually made it easier to work.

After a while the sun came out, and soon it became strong and hot again and the paving stones began steaming. I got so lost in the rebuilding that I didn't really notice anything else, until suddenly I realized the square was really busy, and there was even a crowd standing around watching us.

One of the festival people arrived to set up a sun umbrella for us, and I stood up and stretched. I could feel that everyone was watching and, I don't know why, but I felt the desire to curtsy, so I did, and some of them started clapping, and I grinned, and they clapped louder.

Glimpse Of Light

Zoe pulled on some track pants and a shirt. She resisted looking in the mirror. She'd do the appearance thing later. She wanted to start the day with some yoga, but the studio was too stuffy, and she had to open the windows.

Her studio was on the top story, and the windows looked into a central well in the building, but the sun was just climbing over the roof tops and it was going to be a lovely day. She discovered that the plants in the window boxes needed watering. She liked watering the plants because they felt so refreshed afterwards, so she lingered over the process.

Then the morning paper dropped through the slot in the door, and she picked it up. On the front page was a color picture of someone in front of a sand sculpture. *'Local Sydney artist, Sax Moore and his daughter have been creating a sensation at the Auckland Festival with their sand sculpture.'*

It was Sax from the street, she realized with a start. She took out a tea bag and put it in a cup.

'Winners of last year's competition at Cronulla, their work has been stimulating fierce debate in Auckland, on the nature of art and culture. Renown as a centre of sport and Polynesian culture, Auckland has been having its first Arts Festival since the early 1980's. But the festival has so far lacked a dramatic soul. 'What it found instead was Sax's sculpture in Aotea Square, and over the past few days this has proven a Mecca for office workers and tourists.'

She liked that. It reminded her of the street stuff. The kettle whistled, and she looked at the cup with the tea-bag and realized that she was really just procrastinating about actually starting the yoga practice, and so she rolled out her mat and began.

She felt inspired by the story however and settled straight into the breathing. It was a good practice as a result, and as it developed she found release in muscles that she didn't know she was holding on to. Later, during the relaxation, she felt these same muscles releasing again as she melted into the physical sensations of her body.

The Cake Of History

Adam waited nervously as the news items ticked by. He had a taxi waiting outside, to take him to the Festival Gala, but he needed to catch the Thomas item.

"Despite the rain this morning," the news announcer said brightly, "the controversial sand sculpture project has generated a lot of interest today from the lunch-time crowds." The camera panned over the square until it found Sax in front of the sculpture.

"Art always provokes us to look at our culture, and therefore at ourselves," he said. "New Zealand is an outdoor culture, and here we have an artistic representation of this in the heart of the city, as a centerpiece of the Festival. I think that's what people have been appreciating about the work."

The camera panned over to Sarah. The sculpture was a meticulously crafted beach landscape with a fairy tale castle at one end. Sarah looked so proud, and a big group of onlookers so delighted, that Adam smiled with relief. It was providing just the right images of family entertainment, which the festival charter charged him to provide.

As he got out of the taxi in front of the Concert Chamber of the old Town Hall, he noticed that even at this time there was a few people gathered around the sand sculpture. He savored the interest the event was generating. It should be lit at night, he decided, and they'd have to improve security.

He found Barbara greeting people at the entrance. "The Mayor says well done for the response to Thomas," she whispered. She smiled, and shook her head at his ability to negotiate the art through the stuffiness of the council.

He grinned. "How are ticket sales for tomorrow?"

"They seemed to pick up this afternoon," she said. "The Lloyd Webber musical is booking strongly."

"We make nothing on that though," he said. It was being done by an independent promoter, so it was the rest of the program in which he was more interested.

She nodded. "Everything else is still low. But the dance group is opening with a full house tonight."

"Aucklanders never book in advance," he repeated the conventional wisdom.

They took one another by the arm, and headed into the crush of media, dignitaries, artists, and hangers-on, all of whom seemed to want to get them aside for a few moments.

Sometimes the coincidence of things seemed too much, for just as they found Sax and Sarah by the table of nibbles, Adam saw Councilor Thomas, surrounded by a group of photographers.

"Have you tried the honey almonds?" Sarah asked. Her cheeks were glowing.

Barbara tried some and murmured her approval.

Adam felt an apprehension come over him, then he noticed the Councilor was carrying a child's bucket full of sand and a large sheet of white card. Suddenly the photographers were all around them, and he up-ended the sand into a little pile on the floor, and stuck a plastic beach spade in it at a ridiculous angle. He walked around it, as if assessing its worth, then stopped beside

Adam and opened the card to reveal a mock invoice for some unintelligible sum. The cameras started clicking.

Adam found the experience a rather creative way for the debate to be carried out, and although he was unsettled by the stunt, he started to develop a new respect for the Councilor.

Sarah was standing beside them staring wide-eyed at the performance, not yet understanding what he was doing.

"You should be ashamed of yourself," Councilor Thomas inexplicably suddenly lashed out at her. "Why aren't you in school?"

Tears appeared in her eyes, and she grabbed hold of her father's leg. "It's night time," she told him, her tone suggesting exasperation that such a thing needed explaining, but with a thinness which revealed the vulnerability underneath.

Adam felt his emotions boil in a way that made him want to do something, which he knew if he did, he would regret afterwards, and he thankfully found a moment to step back from the provocation, and realize that the cameras were still clicking. These images of tears on Sarah's face were probably not doing the Councilor's case any benefit, and he allowed the winds of heaven blow around them for a few moments. Then Barbara ushered Sax and Sarah away from the media scrum. He appreciated her professional instincts.

"I think you've made your point Councilor, such as it is, and I'll ask you to please in future be civil to the artists," he said, any respect between them totally disappearing.

Back at home later that night he felt proud of the way he had not reacted in the face of the provocation, and although he should have realized that this was a sign, he accessed the festival's web site from home that night. It was arranged with pages for the program, for reviews and with a gossip page where anyone could have a say.

He clicked through to this page. 'The Festival has got off to a great start,' he began typing, 'with a truck-load of sand, and the concept of sculpture collided with the expectations of one Auckland City Councilor. Art often challenges our expectations, and broadens our sense of who we are, so leave your own comments on this issue here.' He loved the immediacy of the Internet.

Then he checked the reviews. They came through on-line from the paper when they were completed, and the first one was there already; 'Bright young dance company scores hit to open festival' was the heading, and he felt his heart lift with excitement.

He undressed and slipped into bed. He was reading a few pages of 'The Glass Bead Game' each night before he fell asleep. Hesse had such a descriptive style that he found it almost laborious to read, but his vision on the other hand was so light and clear, that it kept pulling him back to read further.

After the events of the evening he had to smile at a section on famous people in history. An old Benedictine Monk was talking to the young hero: "Great men are to youth, like the raisins in the cake of history... It's not so simple as it might be thought, to distinguish the really great, from those who can simply foresee a historical moment, and seize it, giving them a semblance of greatness."

"The fact that an adventurer conquers a kingdom, which may last twenty, fifty, or even a hundred years," the Monk continued, "or an idealist attempts to carry some visionary cultural project to fruition, interests me far less than efforts to establish organizations such as our Order, some of which have endured for a thousand or perhaps two thousand years."

Adam found this somehow comforting. In the face of the chaos and the destructive power of things like nuclear weapons, a two-week festival was only a drop in the ocean, and this perspective helped to give him a sense of detachment from the success or failure of the event, as he drifted into sleep.

Making Sense

"Some things make sense," Sarah told Sax one day. "The sun rises every morning, the tides come and go, I eat when I'm hungry."

Sax nodded. "We love to see the patterns in the chaos we find around us."

"But these things are just natural," she protested.

"Natural to a pattern we have created of how it should be," he told her. "We build patterns to help us make sense out of the world."

"But some things just feel right," she repeated.

"Because we've encountered them before, so we feel familiar with them," he explained again. "But you know, it's really the ones that don't feel right which are more important."

"Why?"

"Because when something doesn't make sense we have to stretch our view of the world to include it."

She sat for a moment and considered this. "Some things don't make sense," she savored the idea, "and this is also important."

Sax Accepts Success

We discovered a rope barrier around the sculpture in the morning, and a security guard stopped us as we made to step over it. "Sorry sir," he told me, "touching isn't allowed."

"We're the artists," Sarah told him. She sounded so proud, and yet the title seemed so absurd, that any heaviness in the interaction immediately disappeared, and he grinned and stepped back, to allow us through. "It's very nice," he said.

"Thank you," I responded, a bit unsettled by the change. Sarah bowed her acknowledgment, and then slipped under the rope before revealing her excitement with a little skip.

The sculpture was largely complete by now and we just had a little retouching work to do, and some tidying up. I connected up the hose and gave the sand a light spray.

To start with the rope gave me the sense of working on a stage, but as the square got busy it became more like a haven, and the security guard was like a new attraction for the public.

I caught Sarah looking at him in a wondering way. I was keeping half an eye on her, looking for any signs of disturbance from last night, but she seemed as buoyant as ever, if perhaps a little more thoughtful.

"So he was making fun of us?" she said, as if reading my mind.

"Who?" I asked, kicking myself at the same time for playing dumb. I felt guilty for exposing her to this sort of thing, I realized, and I was just buying time.

"The man?" Her tone and the brevity of her reply, agreeing that I should give her the benefit of more respect.

I nodded. "Because he thinks it's a waste of money for us to do this."

She considered this.

"I think he's a waste of money," she said. "What does he do?"

"He's part of a group of people who make decisions about how the city will be run." She considered that. That wasn't just anybody, and it had implications. "It's because we're getting successful," I tried to explain, "It attracts the attention of all sorts of people, and some of them are not so nice." I motioned to the security guard. "That's why we get protection."

She grinned, then frowned a moment later. "But the mean man would be his boss."

"Adam will protect us from the mean man," I assured her.

She nodded. She seemed to deal with it all so bravely.

"It's since we started believing in it," she said.

"What?"

"Getting successful."

I acknowledged the correlation between us becoming more successful and our increased faith in it, and for a moment I pumped my ego with the illusion that I was in control. Then I shook my head. "It's not quite that simple."

"Why not?" she asked. "When I said 'it looked silly'

on the first day, you said that if 'we didn't believe in it, no-one would'."

I nodded. I had said that. Perhaps it was that simple. Often we don't listen to our own words of wisdom. The crowds were certainly providing an affirmation that the risks had been worth the effort, and even last night's stunt couldn't dampen that.

Later some characters riding emus appeared over the heads of the crowd. From a distance the illusion was complete, and it was only as they drew closer that I could tell that they were performers on stilts, wearing the costume of the bird's body.

Sarah squealed as soon as she saw them and jumped up to follow the show.

The square was busy and people were sitting eating lunch all around me. I felt like I was in my own island, safe within the rope. I sat and enjoyed the warmth of the sun. It was not too hot today. I had brought my sax, and I took it out of my bag, fitted the mouthpiece and tasted the sound quietly.

In all this activity, and with all the attention, I felt at peace with the world, no need to prove anything, no desire for anything more to occur than what was happening already in my life. I let the notes have their head, and they started small, and then soared above the onlookers and bounced off the walls of the buildings about the square, eventually dying back again to nothing.

I rested the instrument in my lap, and was surprised by applause from the people around me. I had not really been aware of the audience, and I felt suddenly vulnerable and embarrassed.

Sarah was drawn by the noise and she sat down beside me. She loved being the center of attention, and because she loved it, the audience was satisfied and I was able to relax again. I bent over and kissed her on the top of the head.

She shook off my affection. She had a yellow plastic beach spade, and she started drumming it on the ground.

"Where did you get that?" I asked.

"It fell off one of the birds. I'm looking after it for her."

She had a new thought, and clambered to her feet

and scampered over to her castle. She considered it from several sides for a moment, then dug the spade into the top, so it sat at an angle, like some surreal ornament. It reminded me of last night, and then I realized that was her intention and that she was playing with the councilor's protest. I gave her a big cuddle as she sat down.

"It's people inside those birds," she confided in me.

I looked at her as if that was surprising news.

She nodded. "They eat the little things in people's hair."

My eyes grew wider.

She nodded, and I kissed her again on the top of her head.

Like A Flower

Even Adam couldn't quite believe the speed of the media's change in attitude to the sand sculpture. All day he was fielding phone calls from reporters, and even the Herald had come out in support that morning; *'Sand Sculpture Proves Major Tourist Attraction'* ran the headline above a big picture of Sarah, grinning, beside the intricately crafted sculpture.

Beneath the photo was the caption; *'Sand sculpture makes a splash in Aotea Square, despite Councilor's attack on artists (Inset)'*. In one corner of the spread there was a small inset photo of Sarah about to burst into tears under the severe gaze of Councilor Thomas. Adam smiled. He couldn't help it, and although the child in him enjoyed thumbing his nose at the Councilor in this way, the spiritual warrior in him named the emotion 'pride' and warned of karmic results.

'Helped no doubt by the controversy it generated earlier in the week,' the article began, *'thousands of people have turned out to see the sculpture in recent days. Seeing this interest, tour operators have now also started scheduling stops at the square, turning the sand sculpture into what the director of the festival called "a vibrant heart to the festival," Today is your last opportunity to view the sculpture."*

By mid afternoon, word came down from the Mayor that she wanted to see him and he hastened straight up to her office. It was very unusual to be summoned in that way, and despite his sense of success, he couldn't help but worry that there might be something wrong.

"How long is the sand sculpture running," she demanded, as soon as he had sat down and they had exchanged pleasantries.

"It ends today," he assured her.

“That’s what I understood,” she said. "Is it possible to extend it for a few more days?" He absorbed the request. He had been expecting a problem, and it felt like he was in some sort of limbo while he reoriented his attitude. "Business is doing a good trade in the central district for the first time in weeks," she explained.

He grinned, and felt blood rushing to his head. "I'll see what I can do," he told her. "I don't know what other commitments the artists have."

"I'm sure we can find a little more money for your budget, if that's what it takes."

"You're sure we can find...?" It was not a phrase he could recall ever having heard at the Council before.

She nodded.

"I'll see what I can do," he assured her, and he sprang up from the chair, and took his leave.

He took Sax and Sarah out to dinner to celebrate their success. He had a hunch that he should wait for an appropriate moment to broach the topic of an extension, so they went to a burger restaurant on the waterfront, and sat at a window table. The early evening city lights twinkled off the harbor.

Sarah went off to explore the wharf with her angel friend and he let Sax choose a bottle of wine. "The Council will pick up the tab," he said.

"Are they that generous?" Sax was impressed.

"Not normally... But in your case, yes."

"How come?"

"The mayor called me in today, to tell me how much she supports the sculpture."

"Really?"

He seemed suitably impressed, and Adam decided to take the leap. "She wants to extend the season, because it has become so successful."

Sax shook his head, without even thinking about it. "These things have a life," he said.

The immediateness of his response brought Adam to a full stop. He'd sensed a negotiation process was inevitable, but hadn't actually imagined the possibility of outright rejection.

"Already it seems like an unnaturally long time to work on something like this," Sax explained. "We've just been tidying it up today."

"Just a couple more days."

Sax shook his head.

"We can pay you." Adam offered.

Sax shook his head again. "It would lose the magic."

What artist could turn down success and money, Adam wondered, and yet somewhere he understood what Sax was saying, he just didn't want to accept it.

"Part of the beauty is in the transience," Sax explained. "It's like a flower, which we know must wither and die, so we value it all the more while it's fresh and beautiful."

Sarah came skipping back and perched on the edge of her chair. The men sipped their wine in silence for a moment. Adam liked Sax, and would be sorry to see him go. "You'll have to give me your address," he said, "so we can keep in touch."

Sax grinned. "Sarah and I are playing a game which means we might not be home for a while." He glanced at his daughter.

"What game?"

"We have to do everything in new ways," Sarah said.

Adam spied his opportunity. "Would you normally stop, just as your are becoming successful?"

Sax grinned. "Possibly."

"Just one more day?" he begged.

Sax shook his head.

"For an extra thousand dollars!"

"A thousand, for one day?" Sax considered it.

“What’s this?” Sarah was all ears.

“The Mayor wants you guys to keep doing it for another day or two.”

“Go on dad,” Sarah encouraged him. “Why not?”

"Okay," he relented, "one more day, but I fly out Friday morning."

Adam grinned. The food arrived and the conversation wandered in all directions, through a very enjoyable meal.

He called back through the office on the way home and sent off a few e-mails and faxes about the extension to the tour companies and the big hotels, as well as the media, particularly the radio stations, and of course a quick posting on the Internet.

He emphasized how fortunate they had been to been able to extend the season by one extra day, quoting Sax’s ‘It’s like a flower…” response, and concluding that this was absolutely the last opportunity to catch the sand sculpture!

Later he curled up in bed, and read the Glass Bead Game until the early hours. When he finally finished, it left a disappointing taste in his mouth -- the hero leaves the game for new experience, and drowns in a lake while impulsively following new urges.

What did that mean? he wondered. The passion of the young hero to play the game of life, and the important social work achieved at great sacrifice in middle life, sat oddly with the apparent meaninglessness of the final transition, and his mind worried at this as he drifted into sleep.

Foreplay

A taxi truck came to pick up the paintings and, after they had loaded them into the back, Zoe jumped into the cab with the driver. The vehicle had just started to move, when out of the corner of her eye, she suddenly saw Minx leaping on the grass. Her heart stopped and, without thinking she threw open the door, leaped out and ran over to him.

He had a large beetle proudly trapped under one paw. It started wriggling and he leapt back. Immediately it was free, the insect ran for cover, but before it could disappear he pounced again. Zoe was on a mission of rescue however, and she simply grabbed Minx by the scruff of the neck, and ran back to the truck.

"He must have slipped out while we were loading," she said, as they drove off. This produced a grunt from the driver. "How's your day been?" she asked. He grunted again and they lapsed into an stony silence as he negotiated the East Sydney traffic.

Minx snuggled in her lap, and Zoe fondled him behind the ears, while her heartbeat slowly settling down.

The street was deserted at the gallery, there was no answer to the doorbell, and a worn note on the door; 'back in five minutes', which could mean a range of things, which all involved waiting. They unloaded the paintings and stacked them against a lamppost. She felt vulnerable, with her precious work standing out in the street, and she shuffled her weight from foot to foot to relieve the tension. This was not the sort of reception she had envisaged.

She waited for what felt like forever, and when the administrator arrived, he was less than helpful. "It's not strictly within my brief to carry the art," he protested. She bit her lip, and made no comment. She had experimented with some pieces on demolition windows, which were still in their heavy wooden frames, and she needed help to lift them.

Minx bounced around, getting under their feet,

and breaking any sense of formality that the entry to the gallery may have had. She hadn't seen the space empty of other artwork until now and the blank walls looked different from how she'd imagined them. She lit an incense stick and traced along each wall, clearing the energy.

Then she started unwrapping the paintings and placing each one against a wall, just as she had envisaged herself doing, many times. She knew her actions to the smallest detail, and she simply followed her own imagined process. This went so smoothly that she finished hanging the work, with still a couple of hours to spare before the opening, and suddenly she could feel her nerves taking over.

Then she discovered Sax. It surprised her to see him. "I'm a bit early," he said, more excusing the lack of anyone else than his own presence. Even the administrator had disappeared.

"Me too," she said, and they laughed. She felt happy that he had come. “I’ve just finished hanging them.”

He walked about looking at the work as she positioned an adjustable lamp behind one of the window pieces and plugged it in. She turned the switch and stepped back. It was standing in a corner, and, as she hoped, it had the effect of opening the room out into a wider space, and also changing the color of the light.

"You've got some wonderful stuff here," he told her.

She felt herself blush, and giggled. "I'm a little nervous," she admitted.

He nodded. "I know how it is," he sighed.

"I liked what you said about 'everything having a life'," she told him.

He raised his eyebrows.

"There's been a couple of stories about you in the paper."

"I say a lot of things."

"You said, 'Everything has a life.' when you refused to extend the season of your sculpture." Perhaps it was the intimacy of the moment in the empty gallery, or maybe the nerves, but her heart was beating. "That was beautiful." He looked embarrassed, and she laughed. "Very inspiring, really," she assured him, rubbing him on the arm. He shook his head, as if to clear it, and looked like he was going to say something, but thought better of it.

"Do you want to go out for a coffee?" she suggested. “I need to get out until everyone arrives.” He nodded. Minx was asleep in one corner, and so they closed the door on the latch, and she felt better as soon as they got out walking.

They found a nice cafe up in Potts Point.

"You've got a daughter," she prompted him.

"She's staying in Auckland for the weekend, with her mother."

His tone implied a separation, so she didn't need to inquire further. "You flew back today?" she asked, and he nodded. "And came straight to my opening," she said. "I'm honored."

"This is the real reason I couldn't extend the season in Auckland," he told her.

It took a moment for his comment to settle in. She grinned. "You couldn't keep being very successful at a festival, because you had to come to my opening?" She wanted to check that she had understood it correctly.

He looked a bit sheepish and hung his head, which she thought was really cute. He was making her feel very happy.

When they got back to the gallery, it was buzzing with people, and her heart leapt.

The administrator jumped on her. "Where have you been?" he demanded. "Everyone's been asking after you."

She turned to Sax. "You're going to be here for a while?" she asked, stroking him on the arm.

He nodded. "Go for it," he encouraged her.

She kissed him on the cheek, and allowed herself to be sucked into the chaos of introductions and reactions to her art.

Much later, she remembered Minx and spent several worried minutes searching underfoot for him, afraid that he had been spooked by all the people and run away. However, she found him sitting on a table, stretching his head up, to touch noses with Sax. It looked sweet.

She ran her hand over Sax's back and squeezed him on the shoulder. He straightened up, and they stood watching the kitten, while Minx sat and watched them back. Their contact felt so light and comfortable that it felt like meeting an old friend, after all the introductions. She lent her head against his shoulder.

Then Minx leapt into her arms, and she grabbed him and buried her face in his fur. He started purring.

"Is it your kitten?" Sax asked.

She nodded. "I just got him last week."

He smiled. "He's a sweetheart." Then he stretched, and he looked a bit like Minx getting up from the sheepskin. "I think I'm going to go, my body's sore from the plane."

His stretching made her conscious of her own body, and she adjusted the way she was standing. The yoga workshop would be a good way to unwind tomorrow, she thought.

"Maybe we could do something sometime?" he suggested.

"Do you do yoga?"

"I've tried it once or twice."

"It's good for sore bodies."

"Good for making bodies sore." He grinned.

The comment pushed a button in her, but she let it ride for now. "I'm going to a yoga retreat this weekend," she told him, "in Bundeena."

"That sounds lovely," he agreed.

"There's a leaflet about it on the notice board," she said pointing, "if you are interested."

"It could be perfect."

It started to feel awkward between them, and she sensed he was uncertain how to take his leave. To short circuit the dilemma, she leaned over to kiss him on the cheek, but he turned his head so that their lips touched softly instead, and for a moment they looked deeply into one another, before the moist skin parted.

"It was nice to meet you again," she told him, feeling strangely not embarrassed by the intimacy. "Maybe I'll see you at the workshop."

He nodded. "I hope I can make it."

She watched out of the corner of her eye as he found the leaflet, read it, then put it in his pocket.

Read the Wind

I have to make up my mind what I am going to do," one man told another.

"No," the second responded, "you just have to learn to read the wind."

Breaking Free

I slept fitfully and found myself pacing around the apartment in the early hours, just as I had in the bad old days. Zoe was on my mind, and I found her bright eyes twinkling at me, something hypnotic about her gaze constantly drawing me back to examine the memory of that last moment.

The phone rang and, although it was still early, I immediately thought of Sarah, because Auckland was two hours ahead. I jumped to pick it up and was hit instead by the squeal of a fax tone. I punched the start button, watched the paper feed out, and discovered it was from the Adelaide Fringe.

'Dear Sax, I am writing to invite you to be part of this year's Fringe Festival, which starts next week! I was so excited by the response to your sand sculpture in Auckland, that I've talked to the Fringe Board and I've got

a budget to cover your travel and accommodation costs. I can see it working well here in the courtyard to our Fringe Club. I would need you in the first week of the festival to build the atmosphere and it starts on Friday, so I hope this is possible. Call me, so we can discuss this, Trish.'

Somewhere inside me there was a detonation of excitement which I felt would eventually break through my numbness, but for the moment it seemed too much like a crazy dream, and I put the fax in my dairy, where I rediscovered the leaflet for the yoga workshop.

I took it out, read it again, and toyed with it, while I tried to make up my mind what I was going to do. Eventually I became so frustrated with my own inaction that I called the number on the leaflet just to break the impasse, but the phone simply rang and rang, and then a machine answered with a standard message about office-hours. Feeling trapped by the lack of response, I put the receiver down, and continued my pacing.

A bit latter the phone rang again and this time it was Sarah. "How come you're at home?" she demanded.

I wasn't certain what she meant, and I hesitated to respond. "Mmm." I mumbled.

"What about the game?"

I felt a flush of energy and knew she had touched the problem. "I'm just here for a visit," I protested. "I don't usually visit home, so it's okay."

"What are you going to do after your visit?" she pushed me.

"I'm actually going to do a yoga weekend in Bundeena." The need to answer made my mind up for me.

"Where?" she asked, "a what?"

"Never mind," I told her, reasserting my parental role. I considered telling her about the fax from Adelaide, but I hadn't been able to digest it myself yet. "Just checking up on me, are you?"

"Mmmm."

"We'll, I'm good," I lied, "so I'll see you at the airport on Monday morning."

"Can you bring my other school uniform?" she asked. "I've just got the sports one."

"Just as well I'm at home," I reminded her and, having scored my point, I added, "I love you."

I picked up a hire car, and enjoyed the sensation of

getting out on the road. Once I was on the move, I felt a lot better.

The air cleared as soon as I hit the National Park, and I found a turning for Bundeena and followed the winding road through the trees. The sun was streaming down and the green foliage on either side of the road glowed with a joy, which was infectious.

I slowed right down, but it still seemed like no time before I caught sight of Sydney in the distance, rising like a mountain of skyscrapers out of the suburban landscape, and I knew I was almost there.

The yoga center was easy to find, but the workshop had already started, and the room was filled with people and the sound of breathing.

"Use that mat," an attendant told me, pointing to a spare one in the back row. "We'll sort out your registration later."

I hesitated.

"Ever done astanga before?" he asked, and I shook my head. "That's okay, just follow the others." He led me over to the mat. "The important thing is the breathing," he said. "We breathe with a sound in the throat." He demonstrated, and I tried to copy him. After a few moments I found it, it was like a little purring, and he nodded.

"Now, just join in and follow the others," he said. "Each movement has a breath, either in or out, and the breathing is the important thing."

The next time I looked at the clock it had been almost an hour, and despite the fact that my body felt exhausted, I hadn't noticed the time pass. My breath was coming in short gasps now however, and the attendant came over and told me to rest.

I lay back on my mat. I felt like I had climbed a mountain, and I was only too happy to relax. My mind drifted and, although moments later I felt him put a blanket over me, I was already miles away.

I was shaken back to consciousness some time later, and realized that everyone else was packing up their blankets and mats. I felt like I'd woken from a good sleep, and my cares had been lifted. This was both a wonderful feeling, and a slightly worrying one, because I felt different than normal in my body. I packed up my mat and followed the flow outside where everyone was standing in the sun.

Zoe appeared. "You made it."

I nodded. "I arrived late." I felt light-headed, and not very capable of expressing myself.

She rubbed my arm. "You look like you need something to drink," she advised, and she guided me over to a tent in the grounds.

We sat drinking juices, and letting the sunshine soak our muscles with warmth.

"I got a fax from Adelaide this morning," I told her. I had it folded in my pocket, and I took it out and showed it to her.

She read it and laughed. "That's great!"

Her whole-hearted acceptance, swung my opinion in favor of it as well. "Yea," I agreed, and I had a sudden thought. "Why don't you join us?"

"In Adelaide?"

I nodded. "Do some pavement art."

With you?"

I nodded. "I'll tell the Fringe we're three people." I felt like I was blushing, but I may not have been, for she simply looked at me and considered the idea. This took some time. "Maybe think about it," I suggested.

She nodded. "I like the idea."

Anything seemed possible between us.

After dinner we went for a walk. There was a track up the back of the center, and we followed it, sometimes chatting, sometimes silent as we strolled along.

After a time it started getting dark, and the stars came out. I stopped and stared up at a star, which was so bright it must have been a planet.

She stopped beside me, put her hand on my shoulder, and followed my gaze. We stood lost in the majesty of the universe. I could smell her hair, and feel the soft warmth from her touch. Her body softened against mine, and I put my arm around her. Then we turned, and our lips met, and again we were lost in the majesty of the universe.

Then she pulled away. "I don't know," she said.

I nodded. "Maybe it's too fast."

"It's not that," she said. "I've been noticing a pattern. My lovers disappear quickly from my life, while friends remain with me for long periods."

"So you're going to save me from becoming your

lover?" I asked smiling.

She grinned, and twirled around with her arms outstretched. "Yep," she said, and with a twinkle she bounced back the way we had come.

What will Become

A painter had a canvas with which she had been dissatisfied. It was missing something, and she wasn't certain quite how to complete it and the longer she hesitated, the harder it became to make any changes.

Finally she screwed up her courage and added a careful stroke or two, but with every addition the painting changed and she found that more paint was required to complete it. She began to regret that she had embarked on the alterations, for the nature of the work had changed, and some of what she originally had liked was gone.

To fix this, she added more paint and this process continued for some time until finally she began to feel happy with her creation, and yet the original work had now been completely transformed.

Her partner meanwhile was watching the

news. "Any interesting news?" she asked, as she cleaned her brushes.

"Just the normal," he responded, "babies dying at their mother's feet and neighbors killing one another." He looked at her. "How can these things happen?"

In the middle of the painting was a yellow fleck of paint from the earlier incarnation of the work. She had no more of this color and so, in her painting today, she had embellished its prominence.

Then she imagined herself to be that fleck, as the painting was transformed around it, and she felt the danger of the encroaching brush strokes which were obliterating flecks in every direction.

"How can thesethings happen," her partner repeated. "in a world which makes any sense?"

"When I see destruction and creativity so very intertwined in my painting, it makes me think that maybe, in the wider world, this is also what's happening," she told him. "We see the disturbance of the old, but not what will become of it."

Mark in the Rock

Zoe went for a walk before the morning yoga session. She felt tired and sore, but once she started walking, she enjoyed letting her body move and the soreness slowly disappeared. She loved the solitude and the peacefulness of the countryside. She walked for ages through the bush and finally came out onto a flat outcrop of rock, from which she could see over the surrounding country.

It was a wild sight, a sea of green, with patches of black from the bush-fires and blue-ocean in the background. The vegetation looked like it struggled for existence against the harsh sun and the fires, but she knew that it actually relied on the fire, as an important part of the growth cycle. It was weird the way the destruction of the fire promoted growth, she thought.

She put down her bag and took out her sketch-pad

and pens, and as she sat down she noticed marks in the rock and she recognized the shape of a kangaroo etched into the rock-face by her knee. These were aboriginal etchings, she suddenly realized, and she saw the miniature of her life in a much larger context. Her Mambo bag was sitting beside the evidence of people visiting this spot over thousands of years, and her head seemed to disappear in the attempt to conceive of this. Like her, they must have come here to get perspective and record the moment in some way, and she was filled with wonder at the timelessness of the experience. She sat down and filled several pages of her pad, without stopping to think.

Later, as she was savoring a bowl of mueslie and fruit after the morning yoga, Sax sat down on the opposite side of the table.

She smiled. "How's your body today?"

"I had to get in the car this morning, and find a good cup of coffee," he admitted, "then it wasn't too bad."

She grinned. That was so un-cool, she liked it. "You got a car?" she asked, spying an opportunity.

He nodded. "It's a rental... You want a lift back into

town?" She nodded. It was quite intuitive between them. He moved his head and shoulders in various directions. "Now it's all fine," he decided.

"I had a wonderful walk up to some Aboriginal etchings this morning," she told him.

He raised his eyebrows. "You do a lot of physical stuff!"

"I've got a lot of energy," she told him, and she felt an appraising look and a sexual response in her body. "I've decided that I'm not available, if that's what you're thinking."

"I wasn't thinking that."

"Of course not."

"So you have a partner?"

He was cheeky. "No, actually."

"But you're not available."

"Exactly."

They sat with this for some moments, and she felt the need to explain. "Like I said last night, I tend to lose myself in my sexual relationships..." She let it trail off because she really didn't want to get into it. "And what's the big deal with it anyway?"

"Sex?" He shrugged. "It's fun."

"It's just a physical sensation. We can have more intense physical experience with yoga, without all the emotional insecurities."

He nodded. "I get the message."

She blushed.

"I'll get some food," he said. "I'll be back in a moment." He put a book on the table, and wove his way amongst the other people enjoying their food in the sun outside the dinning room.

She pulled the book over, opened it, and browsed through a few pages. It was an exercise book in which he kept a sort of journal with pieces of poetry. She surprised herself delving into his private stuff without asking, but somehow she couldn't help it. The fax from the Adelaide Fringe was inside the front cover and she read it again. She was still reading it when he returned.

"What do you think?" he asked.

She gave a start. "It looks great," she said, feeling she was overplaying the encouragement to hide her embarrassment at being discovered.

"So you'll come with us?"

She stretched, and felt the moment as an energy in her body. "Maybe," she conceded. She found herself changing physically through her yoga and she wanted to extend this to her life, but was much less able to open herself to new experiences.

His eyes lit up, and they turned to their food and ate in silence for some moments, while she absorbed the implications of the project. She did like being with him, and yet she really didn't know him. "So what's your story?" she asked.

He looked at her with wide eyes. "Which bit?"

She giggled. She felt vulnerable having talked about her relationships, and wanted to turn the tables. "Are you in a relationship?" she asked.

He shook his head. "I'm not allowed."

"Why?"

"My girl has impossibly high standards for a new mum."

"That's a cop out." She couldn't let that pass.

He nodded. It was his turn to blush. "I just... I don't really know what I'm looking for in a relationship any more."

She reached out and touched his fingers.

"So I've been withdrawing from them, but now I'm throwing myself out there again." He shook his head. "I don't know."

She grinned. A big white parakeet flew overhead, looking beautiful, but squawking horribly, and they laughed.

"Maybe we could go for a swim on the way back," she suggested, as their fingers gently conversed about the relationship they had said they were not going to have.

She put her bag into his car, and they drove the short distance down to the beach. She pulled off her sandals and let the sand scrunch up between her toes. It was hot, but not fire-dance material. She dropped her towel and pulled off her shirt. She already had her bikini on, and she felt his eyes stroking her again.

He wrapped a towel around himself, and took off his jeans. He looked embarrassed and she felt the urge to whip his towel away, teasing at his silly fears, but she resisted this temptation because it would probably send him the wrong message, until he almost had his bathers on, and then she just had to defrock him. She threw the towel at him, and ran down and into the water.

He pulled his bathers up and chased after her. She just kept running, leaping as far out of the water with each stride so the tide didn't slow her down until she was waist deep, and then she dived under the water. The feel of water on her body aroused her sensuality, and the tumbling in the waves loosened her body.

Boys always wanted to play teasing games, and Sax was no exception. It was just an excuse for physical contact, and she successfully fought him off each time. The teasing contact was exciting her however, and the more they played, the more she lost her inhibitions, and soon they were lost in an embrace.

After a leisurely drive back into town, she directed him to her studio, and he stopped the car outside. They looked at one another, each giving the other space to initiate the next step.

She felt the salt crusty on her skin. "I'm going to have a warm shower," she said.

"That sounds nice."

"Do you want to come up and wash off the salt?"

He nodded.

"I'd like you to see my place," she said.

As Sax turned on the shower the sound of the water echoed Zoe's memory of the slap of the waves. She admired his body through the open bathroom door. He noticed her watching and pulled the shower curtain playfully shut behind him.

Minx stroked around her ankles. She bent down and ruffled the fur under his chin. Then she put on some music, and lit some incense. Normally she would have art lying around in various states of completion, but everything was in the gallery, and the place looked kind of empty.

The sound of the shower water drumming on Sax's body was inviting. She sensed an inevitability about them making love, and finding it more exciting to take the initiative, she stripped off her bathers. "Mind if I join you?" she inquired, stepping through the curtain without waiting for a reply. The water was both refreshing and soothing as it gushed over her skin. She closed her eyes and bathed in the warmth.

"Shall I soap you?" she heard him ask, and she nodded, and felt him rubbing soap over her back. She had a tingling sensation in her neck at his touch and, feeling her nipples become erect, she turned to face the stream of water.

Hours later they wandered down Crown street to the new Sushi Bar. Their bodies now had a familiarity around one another, and several times on the way, they found themselves holding hands.

"Your girl comes back tomorrow?" she inquired as they waited for the food.

He nodded.

"And her mother?" she asked.

"She lives in Auckland... We've been separated for five years."

"You have custody?"

"We don't have a formal arrangement. It just happens that she prefers to live here with me, and that suits me."

They looked at one another in silence for a moment across the table.

"And you?" he inquired.

"I seem to have a pattern of relationships which get more intense, until they blow apart." She felt embarrassed to be revealing this, and couldn't hold his eye contact. "My last ended a few weeks ago."

He reached out and she felt comforted by his touch.

"That's what I was saying last night," she explained.

"Thanks for the warning." He grinned. "Maybe we'll be able to break the pattern.

The sushi arrived on a wooden platter, with a small pile of pickled ginger, and a little bowl of soya sauce. She broke the chopsticks apart, and picked up a piece, dunked it in the soya sauce, and savored the taste. The sweet tang of the ginger mixed with the bite of the wassabi.

Waiting for a Bus

Sarah sat in the sand pit at day-care by herself, while all the other children were running around and playing.

Seeing this a concerned teacher came over.

"Why don't you play softball with the others?" she said. "Or climb on the jungle gym, or read in the library?"

Sarah eyed her with an icy stare.

"Go away," she commanded. "I'm waiting for a bus." And she returned her attention to the subject at hand.

Change in the Air

"There were two other kids going unaccompanied," I told dad, as I got in the car, "and they gave us apple pie for breakfast."

He nodded. "Put your seat belt on."

"I can't." I motioned to the bulge in front of my jacket. "Firefly's asleep in here."

"You carried her like that?"

I nodded. "Right through all the machines that check you, and not one of them found her."

He nodded. "Well you'll have to wake her up now so you can put your belt on." I reluctantly unzipped my jacket and eased her out. She climbed sleepily up onto my shoulder, and then onto the headrest beside my ear.

Dad started the car and drove off. "Actually," he said, "your school uniform is in the back, and we're a bit late, so maybe you should hop over and put it on as we go."

"Cool car," I told him.

"Part of the game," he explained.

I grinned. "They gave us these activity books on the plane, like I got the other time, but these were new ones."

He nodded. "Climb over the back and change," he told me. "I'm going to drop you straight at school."

"Okay! I heard you." I clambered through between the front seats. I didn't like doing this, because I knew that it was bad luck, but his insistence overcame my intuition in the matter.

“I saw this great film in Auckland with mum," I said. He nodded. He wasn't listening. "Mum says you look a lot better."

This got his attention. "Better than what?"

"You know. That she likes you more now."

"Sarah we're not going to get back together," he said in that tone of voice, which always brought something up in my throat, "and will you get your uniform on!"

“Okay!” He wasn’t really listening, and I was looking forward to telling my friends about my adventure, so I slipped the uniform on without another word.

The classroom had that old familiar smell, but I was late and the others were already working in their books, so I went straight to my desk and sat down.

"Where were you last week?" the teacher asked.

"I was working at a festival in New Zealand," I told her, making sure I was speaking loudly, I could hardly get the words out fast enough, I was so excited. She looked at me without responding, and I reviewed my answer to check the information. "I flew back this morning," I added for effect, and to show my best intentions.

"Did you bring a note?" she asked.

I gasped. "I've just come from the airport," I explained, and I cursed dad under my breath for not giving me one. I knew this would happen. I felt in my pocket. “I’ve got my plane ticket,” I announced triumphantly, and the class snickered. "Dad phoned from New Zealand ..." I started to explain, but her look stopped me.

"We received no notification of your absence," she said, "which doesn't show a very responsible attitude.

You can't just take time off whenever you like from school, just because you're going to a festival, or whatever the reason may be."

“Working at a festival,” I explained.

“Working?” she was incredulous. “Doing what?”

“Sand Sculpture.”

“I've talked to you before about these stories that you make up,” she said. “You better see me afterwards.” She motioned me to go and sit down. I knew there was no arguing with her when she was in this mood, and anyway the glances, and smiles from my friends told me that it almost made me more special in their eyes, so I didn't mind.

"They put us up in this really big hotel," I told them in the break, "where there was tables full of every kind of food for breakfast, and you just helped yourself to as much as you want."

They were all wide-eyed, but some couldn't really understand.

"So you just built a sand castle?" one asked.

I nodded. "Like a sculpture. We were a massive success, and we were in the papers and on the television." I let the importance of it all sink in. "Of course it was slow to start with," I admitted, "but I never thought it wouldn't work."

They looked at one another. This was a situation which definitely had some magical overtones, and the power and mystery of it, lent me an added status for the rest of the day.

Dad was waiting after school, and I gave him a big hug.

"The teacher didn't like it, that I was away so long," I told him. "You didn't phone them!"

"Agghh." He cleared his throat. "Was there a problem?"

"Of course there was." I beat his arm with my fists, until he had to grab me and stop me. I cuddled against him. "You have to call the teacher," I told him.

"Okay." He let go and we walked off, making it most of the way down the street in silence, which was unusual.

I took his hand. "Have you got your period?" I

asked, because my friends had said about their mums feeling grumpy when they had their period. I hadn't heard about it for dads, but it would be sexist to think that dads didn't do it too.

He grinned. "No, as it happens I haven't," he said, but there was a twinkle in his eye which told of further secrets. "I've met someone who I want you to meet."

The way he said it sounded dangerous. "Not another girlfriend," I scolded him.

He nodded bashfully, and I slapped him on the arm. "You promised never again?" I said.

"I never did."

"You did."

He shrugged.

"What's her name?"

"Zoe."

We walked in silence. I knew I shouldn't have climbed between the seats this morning. It was bringing nothing but trouble.

Zoe sat at the table opposite me. She put a sketchbook and a box of pens in front of her, opened the book and the box and arranged the pens on the table around the pad. Her hands were beautiful, and she touched each pen like it was a special friend.

"Do you want to do some?" she asked, seeing my gaze.

I felt determined to make it hard for her to like me, but drawing was one of my favorite things, so I nodded.

She tore out a page, and gave it to me and I sat wondering what to draw for some moments. Firefly was lying beside me on the table with her legs spread in a suggestive pose. Zoe hadn't discovered her yet, and Firefly was taking the opportunity to be cheeky.

I giggled at her antics, at which Zoe looked at me, and I bent my head over the paper and drew some random lines. This only encouraged Firefly, who threw her nose up and strutted about, till I giggled again.

Dad came over. "We eat in ten minutes," he said. He stood staring down at our drawings for a moment. I kept working and avoided looking at him. He ruffled my hair. I hated it when he did that. “Can you help me for a moment?” he asked Zoe and she got up and they went into the kitchen area together.

A kitten pounced on my shoelace. I reached down to

stroke it, and it jumped straight into my lap and started purring. It was so fluffy that it's face got lost, and I stroked the fur away from its eyes.

"You can tell by little things," I explained quietly. "Like the way she looked at him when she answered the door, and then they kissed on the lips." I scratched behind his ears. "And like the way he went straight into her kitchen and started cooking dinner!"

Zoe came back and sat down. "I see Minx has found you," she said. There was an awkwardness between us, but I was glad that at least she wasn't trying to be my friend in that false way that adults have sometimes.

"Mmm," I said, at which the kitten stretched and dug its claws into my leg, and I jumped in surprise. It leapt down and walked away as if that is exactly what had been intended.

"What's its name?" I asked.

"Minx."

I looked around. I liked her studio, with its faint smell of paint and I began to warm to her, despite my best intentions.

Zoe made up a bed on a mattress in the corner and

dad read to me from a book I had got at school. I was really too big to be read to like this, but it was one of our favorite things and I was exhausted and enjoyed the cuddle. I snuggled my head on his shoulder.

"We've been invited to work at the Fringe Festival in Adelaide," he said when he had finished.

"When?" I asked, yawning.

"Probably drive over on Wednesday," he said.

That was soon. I shuddered when I thought what the teacher might say, but I knew my friends would be pleased to discover that things were still moving along with the magic of the sand sculpture.

"So you will either have to take more time off school," he said, stroking my hair, "or we could find someone for you to stay with for a week, while we're away."

I nodded. I could always stay at a friend's house, but going to Adelaide sounded fun, whatever reservations my teacher may have, and I felt drawn into conspiracy with, what I began to think of as dad's irresponsibility.

"Who's we?" I suddenly wondered.

"Zoe does pavement-art," he told me, "she's coming to work with us."

Suddenly I was wide-awake and I realized then that I had to go to Adelaide, because I couldn't let him go alone with her. "You'll have to give the teacher a call," I told him firmly, "and organize it properly this time."

He nodded, and got up and tucked me in. Firefly was asleep on the pillow beside me, and Minx crawled up onto the bed and snuggled on my tummy. I could feel his purring through the blanket, so I felt safe in this strange place, but despite my exhaustion I lay away for ages before I could get to sleep.

The Other Side

A clown approached a woman sitting in a wheelchair in a public place where there were no chairs.

"You're so lucky," the clown said.

The woman looked at him angrily. Used to sympathy for her disability, she assumed he was making fun of her. "I've got a spinal problem," she felt compelled to point out. "Which causes me intense pain, if I don't take medication."

"I'm very sorry to hear that," the clown responded, looking genuinely distressed, but then he brightened again. "But on the other side, you're so lucky to have a chair to sit in."

The Axe Falls

By the second week of the festival Adam had begun to allow himself a morning swim before work and he arrived in on Wednesday, relaxed and energised from 20 laps, to find a request from the head of Recreational Services for a meeting.

Barbara was on the phone and she just shrugged when he looked at her for explanation. “He said just go straight up,” she told him, covering the mouthpiece and gesturing to indicate she knew nothing more.

He wondered what it might be about as he waited for the lift. It looked like they would meet box office targets by the weekend but it was still a little early for a promotion. He marveled at how things changed so easily. The festival had been struggling to justify itself in the first week, and now it was a 'natural success', and the image of this success rewrote the history of the first week, so that it might never have been.

"As I understand it, the festival is going very well," the boss began, "and you are to be congratulated for your excellent work."

"Thank you."

"However, this makes it even harder for me to perform my duty today..." There was an awkward pause. "As I must tell you that a restructuring has occurred in the Department, and that your position has been abolished." He looked at his hands. The words made no sense to Adam. "You will, of course be kept on full wages, until an equivalent position can be found for you within the Council," the boss added, "however I've been asked to request that you clean out your desk today, and take leave on full pay."

Disbelief flowed over Adam. "But I have a contract." The only grounds on which he knew that they could cancel it was on 'inadequate performance of duties'. "And you just said it was going well."

He nodded. "Your contract allows for restructuring, and you will be retained at your current seniority in another position."

"Another position?"

"Of similar seniority."

"In Recreation?"

The boss shrugged. "I don't know."

"Or maybe Rubbish Disposal, or Traffic?"

"I don't know. I'm sorry Adam, it wasn't my decision." He looked down at his hands again. "It's what I've been instructed to do."

Adam had no response to fall back on. "But what about the festival?" he couldn't believe it.

"They are obviously going keep it going." He was trying to sound encouraging. "I think they're going to set up a separate department."

Adam realized that all the work he had put in was just going to be subsumed into the system, and that he had no rights to any of the fruits of his labour.

"Naturally, should you wish to leave, we'll give you an excellent reference," the boss said, "and mention the extraordinary success of your work."

"Naturally," Adam repeated almost mindlessly. "Extraordinary."

His emotions were in turmoil as he waited for the

lift. It took ages to arrive and, as more people gathered, the prospect of the confined space became less inviting and he finally took the stairs instead.

It felt good to move his body.

He had an oppressive sense that he must have done something wrong, and he reviewed the meeting again in his mind for clues. Then he reviewed all the confrontations he'd had in the past few weeks, to find his mistake. Was it Kundera, or was it Kafka, who had pointed out that the punishment seeks out the crime? Adam was busy seeking his, as his feet pounded down the stairs.

He blurted out the news as soon as he reached the office, and then he looked around the room, half taking it in for the last time, and half trying to decide where to start packing.

He must have been swaying unsteadily, for Barbara came running over and put her hands on his shoulders. He looked at her, and realized how in shock he must be because there didn't seem any way forward from that point, anything to say, any action to take, and he was conscious of his breath. It was very tight.

Then she pulled him to her and the warmth of her body was comforting. He relaxed his neck so his nose pressed into her neck. Her skin was warm and soft. They had an occasionally physical relationship, seeking comfort from one another in times of crisis, and this was one of those times. Her touch slowly revived him.

"I'm going to phone the Mayor," he decided.

"And say what?"

"Find out how it happened, anyway," he said. He half hoped that the decision could be reversed and he felt sure she would spring to his aid.

"Go on then."

He picked up the phone. He had nothing to loose. It rang at the other end and he had a moment of panic, wondering what he was going to say, before her voice answered.

"Good morning."

"Good morning Mayor, it's Adam from Recreation."

"Good morning Adam."

There was warmth in her voice, which encouraged him. "I've just had a meeting with the head of Recreation," he told her, leaping in and feeling better for it. "He tells me my position has been abolished!" He still couldn't believe it, and the tone of his voice obviously reflected this.

There was an in-drawn breath on the other end of the phone. "Has it happened that quickly?"

"Were you aware that it was being axed?" he asked.

"I'm sorry, but I wasn't able to protect you," she told him. "You'd made some pretty powerful enemies with the style of the festival, and I didn't have the numbers on that committee."

It sounded like an excuse, and he was left with a feeling that he had been used. "And that's all there is to it?"

"That's politics... You've got to remember that you've also made some powerful friends," she reminded him, "and these will put you in a good position later on, if you play your cards right."

"I understand," he said. "Thank you."

"Best of luck, Adam."

He put the phone down. He realized that he just had to walk away from it, and he started sorting through the stuff on his desk. "It's just the politics," he tried to explain to Barbara.

She was sitting on the edge of her desk, watching him. "You should go up to Corromandel and have a break," she advised. "I've got a friend you could stay with. They're having a dance-party in a week or two and I know they would appreciate some help."

As one door closes, another opens, he told himself, however he had to struggle against a heaviness in his movements, as he packed his bag.

"You should definitely take a break," she repeated.

He looked at her. "I think it's become compulsory," he said and they laughed. It felt good to laugh, but the hysterical tinge was unsettling.

"I mean have a real holiday, and enjoy yourself."

He nodded, but he was still wrestling with the feeling that it must be a punishment for not doing it properly in some way, and so a holiday sounded weird.

"Do you want to come over to my place later?" she asked.

He nodded. "Thanks."

As he waited for a taxi, all his personal papers in a couple of boxes beside him, he wondered what he was going to do with the rest of the day, or with tomorrow, and he saw his life stretching before him, and found it suddenly dangerously open and vulnerable.

Behind him, the square was full of people and the festivities, and this provided an ironic backdrop to his personal drama. It would all simply go on without him, he realized, and he had a moment of insight where he saw how much his ego was attached to being the person who was making it happen. Then he felt a strange surge of relief from this responsibility, and he became dizzy and sat down on one of the boxes.

A taxi pulled up, but he waved it on.

He felt so light-headed it was scary and he had to just sit and allow the flow of experience until he calmed down. After a while this allowed him to enjoy the festival atmosphere for possibly the first real time. It was a beautiful day and the atmosphere in the square was full of joy and surprise.

Later, as the bustle of the lunch hour started to subside, he began to grow depressed again, and he realized he was in shock, and he hailed a taxi and went home.

He put on some incense and tidied up his favorite meditation space. He was so thankful to have this practice at times like these. If only everyone realized how valuable it was, he thought, or perhaps it was only because he had these sorts of things happening in his life that he had to do it. He smiled at himself. There was the monkey-mind again, busying itself with riddles to avoid the physical.

He crossed his legs into lotus posture, sat with the spine erect and focused on the sound of his breath.

When he had found the peace of mind to calmly survey his position, he began to see it as an opportunity, and he decided that Barbara was right and a clean break would be good. While he had some money however, he reasoned that he may as well make use his time to look at new opportunities and so he phoned Trish at the Adelaide Fringe.

"Hi, it's Adam calling from Auckland."

"How's everything going?" she asked.

It was an innocent question, but it threw him into a dark pit without an answer. "The festival's going well," he managed, but I'm coming over to Adelaide tomorrow, and I'm looking for work."

"How come?"

"It's a long story," he said, struggling against a sense of failure. "I think I'll have to explain when I arrive."

"I'll get you a gold pass to the Fringe, anyway," she told him. "That will get you into any show free on the opening night, and also into the Fringe Club."

"Fantastic."

"I'll give some thought to work," she said, "but I wouldn't hold your breath at this stage. Lots of voluntary work, of course."

"That's possible," he said.

“Come to the office when you get here. We'll see what we can do.”

“Thanks.”

He pressed the tab on the phone to break the connection. His eye fell on the ‘Glass Bead Game’ on the table. Joseph's life had gone through some major transitions, and in allowing them had been strengthened in the process. He sighed at the miraculous guidance that seemed to be always right there when he needed it.

Getting Involved

I dropped Sarah at school, caught a bus down to Circular Quay, and ordered a tea at one of the outdoor cafes. The bustle of the morning flowed around me, as I absorbed the energies of my new relationship. I felt like my body was charged, and I was content to sit and allow the world to flow by.

A clown started working a short distance away. She had a Chaplin-like character, her pants were too large and her jacket was too small, and she held an open sun-umbrella in one hand. She was playing with the way people were walking, following behind them and imitating them, and the normal flow of people about her was affected as people became aware of her game. She started followed close behind someone, her lips pursed, so that when they turned to investigate what the laughter from the bystanders was about, they at first jumped back in fright, and then laughed at their own foolishness for being frightened by a clown trying to kiss them. She repeated this several times, to good effect. People had stopped to watch, forming a small audience and they broke into smiles at the playfulness she was introducing into the otherwise normal reality.

I sat marveling at the tenacious nature of art, that it should manifest even here between a ferry terminal and a train station, almost like the moss, which grows in cracks in a rock face with little visible nourishment. I took out my journal and opened it at a blank page.

Some time later Zoe sat down at the table. I leaned over and kissed her. "How's it going?" I asked, as casually as I could, given the emotions that she was stirring inside me.

She shook her head. "There's been none sold yet." She had been to check on her exhibition.

"It's only been a couple of days," I reminded her.

She nodded.

The clown had developed a sizeable audience, with people watching from many vantage points. I tried to draw Zoe's attention to the performance, but her mind was elsewhere, and, although she looked in that direction, she registered no response. Sarah was like that, often in her own world.

“Sarah seems to have taken to you,” I observed.

“You think so?” She seemed surprised.

I grinned. “Well there hasn’t been any kicking or screaming.” She smiled thinly, not buying into my light hearted attitude, and I began to regret bringing the topic up.

"I don't know if it’s so good," she said, "taking kids out of school." I was surprised by the sudden turn in the conversation and was lost for a response. She kicked my foot playfully under the table. She was wearing sandals and had a silver ring on one of the toes, which accented her physicality. "I love the irreverent attitude to reality that you have," she said. "I find it charming." She flashed me a grin. "But you can't bring up kids that way."

"It's good for them to have variety.” Even to me, my protest sounded hollow. I hoped that she wasn't one of these people who have no children of their own, but always know what's best for other people's children. "I found school stifling," I tried again, "and I think she'll learn more coming with us, than she will by staying here."

She shrugged. "I don't feel comfortable taking her."

I couldn't believe this was really an issue, after knowing one another just a few days. "I'm inviting you as an artistic partner," I told her, "not as a foster parent." I wanted to short-circuit the discussion.

"It's hard to separate the roles," she said, looking down. "It feels like you guys have just moved in."

My heart leapt to my mouth, and I wanted to say something but didn't know what. This wasn't going well.

"Sarah and I are playing a game," I tried explaining, "which is a bit like a spiritual practice, based on the premise that we won't do things that we normally do." She looked interested. "So I can understand that it seems to you like we've just moved in on you in an unnatural way."

"When did you start this?"

"Just before we met, that first time in the street."

She grinned. "You're out there," she said. Her eye caught the clown, and she watched her for some moments.

I had an idea. "Perhaps I could invite you to spend the night at my place," I suggested. "Since that would also be something new."

She nodded hesitantly. "But maybe it's better that I don't come to the Fringe," she suggested.

I shrugged. I really wanted her to come, and there hadn't been a hint of this earlier. "Has something happened?" I asked.

She pouted her lips, and took a sip of coffee. "I guess it's the build-up to getting the exhibition up, and afterwards it all feels a bit flat... Maybe it's that. Sometimes it feels like it's all just an ego exercise, rather than something which breaks the cultural mold or gives anyone a new look at themselves."

"Sounds like a perfect reason to come with us, give you a new challenge, experimental collaboration to throw your art in a new direction, and lots of other art to refresh you."

"Of course you're right." A short black expresso coffee arrived for her.

"Can I have another herb tea?" I asked the waiter.

She took a sip of the coffee, and a thin line of froth sat on her lip like a mustache. She licked it away.

"When you put so much work into something," I agreed, "it's natural to re-evaluate."

She nodded, and a bright smile cut through her heavy feeling. "You fancy yourself as a bit of a sage, don't you?'

That seemed unfair, because I was just trying to relate to her. "Maybe" I said, and I found myself sounding a little coy.

"I think I'll go and browse through the Museum of Contemporary Art," she decided.

"Good idea," I agreed.

She swung back the rest of her coffee in one hit, and stood up, her body moving effortlessly on the impulse. "Do you want to come?"

I shook my head. I thought it was best if she went by herself. "You go," I told her. "I've go t tea coming." She bent over and rested her forehead on mine. Then our lips met. Nothing else mattered.

"I'll see you back here," she told me.

I nodded and watched her walk away.

Then, looking down at the table, I noticed that I had been writing something in my journal as we had talked: 'The act of faith required to take new steps becomes both harder, and easier, as we progress.'

My heart missed a beat. I was talking to myself in riddles now. That scared me, and I wondered if I was getting a little too far 'out there', as Zoe had described it.

I drew comfort however from the fact that some part of my subconscious, or perhaps some higher power, was sending my conscious mind signals of a larger perspective.

Striking Out

Adam got an early flight into Adelaide and it was only mid-morning by the time he had checked into the hotel and had a shower. He decided to explore the city. It was good to get out and walk, to use the movement to free his mind from its constant questioning. He was like that in new places anyway, he needed to get out and roam to establish the territory.

Today he found himself observing his surroundings more than usual in an effort to avoid each footfall becoming the unconscious mantra: "Why? Why?" The area around the hotel was like a red-light district and there were hustlers at some of the doors.

He crossed a main road and entered a pedestrian mall, lined with department stores and fashionable shops. He passed several street-shows with good-sized crowds even at this early hour. He wanted to stop and enjoy them, and he lingered for a moment, but he was too restless to immerse himself in the cultural feast just yet, and he kept moving.

After a while the street became a more bohemian area, with craft shops and cafes. His only plan for the day was to go to the Fringe office and pick up the pass to the festival, and with nothing else to fill his time, he finally stopped for a coffee. He had booked his flight in the first flush of release, and now he began to wonder exactly what he was doing here.

This feeling of dislocation was reinforced when he got to the Fringe office, by the long queue at the information desk. There was only one person serving and a string of university students in front of him was each looking for information on their particular interest. Behind him, a woman with brightly died hair and large boots, kept turning to the businessman behind her for support in her outrage at the delay. He just stood impassively waiting his turn, not keen to buy into her theatrics. Further on a couple of old ladies were happily chatting away. They were on an outing, and didn't care how long it took.

"I think Trish has left a pass here for me," he said to the woman, when he finally got to the front. "I phoned her yesterday from Auckland."

"Your name?"

"Adam Simonds."

She looked through a drawer behind the desk, then shook her head. "I can't find one." She was tired and abrupt and he wanted to slink out the door at this new rejection, but he stood his ground.

“Could you check with her?" he asked. She gave him a look, which made him conscious that he was holding up the whole line, and reluctantly went to ask.

He picked up a Fringe program from a pile on the desk and leafed though it. It was newspaper format, crammed with listings and adverts, so densely full of information that it felt like it was going to be difficult to find his way around it.

Finally she came back waving a pass, and handed it to him. She smiled, it had been worth her while and he was forgiven. He thanked her, and shuffled quickly out of the way, not daring to ask if there was any message from Trish, as she turned to the lady in the boots. Not knowing what to do next, he felt even more alone and he stood clutching the pass and the program. His mind was full of thousand different thoughts all competing for his attention, and he knew that he desperately needed to meditate.

He found a quiet, shady place in the park beside the river Torrens, and crossed his legs into lotus posture. His knees were stiff and the discomfort of the posture helped bring his awareness into his body. He straightened his back, released his shoulders, and felt the rise and fall of his chest as the breath passed in and out.

Then he closed his eyes and brought his awareness to the feeling of the air moving through his open lips, remaining conscious of this sensation, and allowing all else to be. At first, he was very aware of a hubbub of thoughts, and every now and again one would demand attention and he would let it go. This always happened, but today more than ever, and he had to sit longer before he began to feel at peace with himself.

Slowly this feeling extended outwards until he felt at peace with the world around him, able to allow the sensations and his place in them without any sense of fear, desire, or control of the experience.

He had dinner that evening at a café by the Fringe office. It was a hot evening and the town was buzzing. Afterwards he was enjoying a coffee and making another attempt at the program, when someone stopped by his table and he looked up to see Trish. He grinned, unspeakably happy to see a friendly face.

"Mind if I join you?" she asked. She was holding a tray of food.

"Please," he managed to grunt.

She sat down. "Sorry I couldn't see you this morning, I was in a meeting."

He shrugged and she started eating without any ceremony. "How's it going?" he asked.

"Never well from someone's point of view." She sighed. "Some shows lose money, and they like to blame someone."

He grinned "Tell me about it!" She took another mouthful of food and chewed impatiently. He felt that the relationship between them was different than in Auckland, but he couldn't say exactly what it was. He gestured to the program. "What would you suggest that I see tonight?"

"I'm going to 'the Mother of all Clowns' at eleven in the Fringe Club. She's a great female stand-up comic."

"And in the early time-slot?" He had worked out that there were two or three sessions in most venues each evening.

"Your pass will get you into every show in the Fringe tonight so there's quite a bit to choose from." She considered the options, as she continued eating. She couldn't even stop eating to think, and he recognized this impatience with the mundane day to day things when so much was to be done, and was now painfully aware of the emptiness when this sense of importance was taken away. He realised this was the change in the dynamic between them. "What do you like?" she asked.

"Maybe some dance."

"Go and see the 'High Flyers' in the Myer Centre," she decided. "They're doing something suspended on ropes in the central atrium."

"Where's that?"

"That's the big department store in the mall," she

told him, and then almost without a pause for breath, "So what happened in Auckland?"

He had been dreading the question, because he didn't know how to explain it, but she had sprung it on him so that he had no time to formulate his thoughts. "I got caught in the politics," he found himself saying. "You remember that councilor who was stirring trouble over the sand sculpture?" She nodded. "He was a member of a committee looking into restructuring of the Recreation Department." He gave her a moment to imagine what might have occurred. "The committee made my position redundant."

A look between sympathy and terror crossed her face. "But don't you have any job security?"

"I'm still on full pay." He shook his head to express his personal lack of comprehension at the flow of events, even as he tried to explain it.

"So you are getting paid to enjoy our festival?" she said.

He nodded.

"You're lucky," she decided. "You won't want me finding you any work then while you're here then?"

“It’s not so much for the money,” he said, feeling the weight of empty time on his hands.

She nodded. “Let me know if you need something to keep you busy.” She sighed. “There’s always plenty of that.”

He grinned. Not always, he was discovering.

When he found the department store, it had a high central atrium with ground floor cafes and a roller-coaster suspended five floors above in the roof. There were ropes hanging from the tubes of this ride, and people were suspended on two of these. They each had their feet on the pillars, which ran from floor to ceiling supporting the building, so that they stood parallel to the floor facing down.

The figures were perfectly still and nobody was paying them much attention, so Adam sat at a table at one of the cafes, and ordered a lemon-grass tea.

Moments later, the atrium lights dimmed and spotlights came up on the figures, who started moving, so that they appeared to be walking down the pillars towards the floor. The escalators were still full of people going about their shopping, alongside this impossibility of walking on the wall, and this simple illusion twisted Adam's perspective on the building and made him question his basic assumptions about reality. He liked that. It seemed to also be speaking to his individual situation.

He realized he had been nurturing a sense of injustice at his treatment in Auckland and, from this new perspective, it was nothing but an opportunity and he finally allowed himself to bathe in the unique experience of the Festival.

To Allow Myself

"I find that it's such a big effort to do anything," a successful person told a friend, "that I really have to want to do whatever it is."

"But you always seem to do what you want," the friend responded.

That's what I'm saying," the first snapped back, "and I'm explaining what a big effort it is to allow myself to do that."

Risk Beyond Belief

Zoe had been stacking stuff by the door for the journey, and she added a bag of clothes to the pile. She rarely traveled and she felt excited, and yet unsettled, by the departure process. She picked up an empty cardboard box and took it into the kitchen.

"Boo!" Sarah jumped out from behind the bench.

Sax was picking up a hire car, and the girl was behaving very differently without him around. At any other time, it might have been fun, but now it was just an annoyance.

"Go and make sure you've got your things packed!" Zoe told her.

"I have already," she protested, "three times!" She flounced off with a strange look in her eye.

Zoe started loading the box with some food for the road, and as soon as she opened the refrigerator, Minx rubbed against her ankles. He stood on his hind-legs, begging to be lifted up, and he was so sweet, that she had to oblige. "Yes, we're taking you," she told him. "Don't worry." He licked her nose and the sensation was strangely rasping in contrast to the sweet little face. She let him scramble up and sit on her shoulder, as she carried the box over to the door, and placed it with the other stuff.

She counted the bags and stopped. She could have sworn she had put her chalks there already, but now her street-bag was nowhere in sight. She checked behind the door where it belonged, and discovered her memory of having moved it was correct, and she had a moment of panic.

Then she reasoned that she must have put it somewhere else, and she put Minx down and looked methodically through the studio, growing frustrated, as she found no trace of it.

Finally she checked the door one last time and suddenly found it, where she knew it hadn't been, just a few minutes before. There was only one explanation. Sarah had been skulking around during the search, and now Zoe caught a sly smile crossing her face, which told the rest of the story.

“I don't have time to play hide and seek with you," she exploded. "Leave my stuff alone!"

Sarah looked very innocent.

"Don't pretend you don't know what I'm talking about!" The louder Zoe's voice became, the more innocent Sarah's look became, and of course, just at that moment, Sax came back from picking up the car.

"Why blame me?" Sarah demanded, flouncing over to her bed and throwing herself on it, in tears.

Sax looked from one to the other, at a loss.

Zoe shrugged. "I think she needs a parent to look after her," she said drily.

She began to feel better once they got over the Blue Mountains and out onto the open highway. It felt like it was going to be a scorcher of a day, but at this early hour, it was quite pleasant with the breeze in the open window.

It had been hard to get away, and there was still an awkward feeling in the car. Sarah was curled on a pile of bags and blankets in the back seat, not really asleep, but at some low level of semi-consciousness. "I want to get in the front," she said, for the thousandth time, sensing Zoe's attention.

Zoe looked back to the road ahead. Minx was asleep in her lap, and he stirred and stretched at the touch of the wind, and then nuzzled his face back into her stomach. She wished she could stretch like that, feeling the confines of the vehicle.

"I'm going to do a practice, when we stop for food," she announced. She turned to Sax. "Maybe you want to join me?"

He pursed his lips as if savoring the idea, then nodded. "Okay," he agreed. He took his eyes from the road long enough for their contact to share the joy of the adventure, and she put her feet up on the dashboard and released herself to the journey.

"I want to get in the front seat," Sarah said again.

"Okay, okay," Zoe conceded, "We can take turns."

It quickly grew hot and by mid-day it began to feel almost unbearable, as if they were baking in an oven.

The countryside out here was so monotonously flat, that it always looked the same, giving the impression that they were rattling along and still making no progress at all. It did something funny to the mind, and Zoe wasn't sure she liked it, but the sensation of movement did free her to rove in her imagination, which she liked.

She leaned towards the open window and the wind on her face seemed to almost burn, but any breeze was better than none.

Out of nowhere a big hamburger sign appeared, looking incongruous in this near desert landscape. A neon sign declaring 'Air-conditioned' was flashing on and off, even in this glare.

Sarah leaned forward between the seats. "I need a drink!" she pleaded hoarsely.

"Okay!" Sax told her. He slowed down and turned off the road into the parking area of the rest-stop.

"Drink," Sarah chirped happily, as they parked.

Zoe opened the door, and Minx leapt out and she followed. It was good to finally get out, and she stretched, opened the back door and grabbed a towel. "Remember we're doing some yoga," she said.

Sax nodded, but Sarah looked crestfallen. "Drink?"

she pleaded.

"Do some with us." Zoe wanted to include her.

"I don't want to!" Sarah was suddenly angry. "I want a drink!"

Sax looked pleadingly at Zoe, to silence any further comment, then gave Sarah some change and she skipped off.

"You spoil her when you give in like that," she told him.

They found a shady spot on the grass.

"You're threatening to her," he explained.

"I'm threatening?"

"Just give her time to accept it."

“What?”

“Our relationship.”

“Ahh.” She suddenly remembered Minx, couldn't see him anywhere, and had a momentary panic attack, before spying him clinging to a small tree. As the fear of loosing him released from her throat, she had a sudden idea and, scooping him up, she ran after Sarah.

As she stepped inside the building, there was a rush of cold air from the air conditioning, as the doors closed behind her. "Sarah!" she called, spying the girl.

Sarah turned, and the look on her face was set in refusal of any delay to her plans.

"Could you look after Minx, so she doesn't get lost?" Zoe asked.

Sarah softened and she reached out and took the kitten, hugging him like a favorite doll. Minx reached up and nuzzled into her face, purring, and she laughed.

“I don’t know that you’re allowed to take him in the restaurant area officially,” Zoe said, “so you may need to hide him when you go in.”

Sarah smiled and slipped him under her shirt. “I’ll keep him in here with Firefly.”

“Good,” Zoe said, and Sarah scampered off.

It wasn't until she got into the rhythm of the breathing that her mind stilled. They took the work slowly, because of the heat, but they were sweating from the moment they started.

Sax looked ungainly as he attempted to do some of the postures, and sometimes she had to stop herself from laughing at his attempts at contortion. "This is so good for you," she told him, when they paused for a moment.

"That's why I'm sweating like a pig."

"That's the toxins being purged from your muscles."

He nodded.

"Don't worry about getting the body right," she told him, "just surrender to the breath."

He grinned. His shirt was clinging to his body, and she threw him the towel so he could rub himself down.

Sarah waved from one of the tables when they got inside. Minx was safely asleep on her lap, and Zoe gave her an appreciative look. Sarah accepted it graciously and motioned to her father to sit in the chair beside her.

Seeing the interactions with new eyes, Zoe tried to make space for the precocious behaviour of the girl. The yoga had given her a physical sense of peace, but she couldn't help wondering whether it had been the right decision to join these two in their adventure.

Sarah leapt into the front seat as they prepared to get back on the road. Her stomach was full, and she was much happier.

"I'll drive this shift," Zoe said. Sax gave her the keys and got into the back seat, and she started the car and eased it back out onto the highway.

"Let's play a game?" Sarah said.

"I spy?" Sax suggested.

Zoe noticed Sarah go to nod, then consider briefly. "No. I want to play ten questions," she said.

"What's that?" Zoe asked.

"It's one Sarah made up," Sax explained.

"I'll tell her," Sarah told him. "You think of something, and you say what sort of thing it is. Maybe it's a film, or a book, or a country, or anything, and then you have to find out what it is. And you've only got ten questions, and I can only say yes or no."

"Who says yes or no?" Zoe teased her.

"The person that's in." Sarah looked at her for a moment. "Okay? You start."

Zoe could feel the struggle between them. "No, you start," she played into the game.

The rest of the day was like an endless sauna, punctuated by deserted small settlements which each seemed to straggle out on either side of the pub, the post office and the service station.

The only thing that made it bearable was the

driving, because she enjoyed the physical coordination required to control the vehicle.

She drove until it started to get dark, and then she took the back seat and had a sleep.

She slept fitfully with the hot wind playing in her dreams, and it wasn't until well after midnight that it started to feel cooler, and she awoke again.

She leaned out the window to let the air blow away the cobwebs, and looked up into the vast canopy of stars above them. The sky was rich with points of light, without all the lights which normally got in the way, and the enormity of it was awesome.

"Traveling always puts things in perspective," Sax said for no apparent reason, but articulating almost exactly her own thoughts.

"Like the stars," she agreed, ducking her head back inside the vehicle. "You realize what a small part you play in the whole thing."

He nodded, catching her eye in the mirror. "Which makes it easier to keep doing it, somehow."

She nodded. She leaned forward and rested her chin on his shoulder, then turned her head and brushed his neck with her lips. She was in unknown territory, but the physical connection between them gave her strength.

Consummation

I rolled out of bed and immediately encountered tightness in my muscles, and sat back down on the edge of the bed. Minx was curled asleep on Zoe's stomach and he awoke at my movement and stretched, before nuzzling back into the bedclothes. The movement looked so enjoyable that I also wanted to stretch, but the tightness was stronger than anything I had experienced before, and instead I stumbled into the bathroom and thawed out under the warm shower.

Driving long distances was always bad for my body, but this felt like I had a skeleton which was several sizes too small, and I realized that it must be the yoga. Zoe came into the bathroom, as I was finishing. "I feel terrible after that yoga yesterday," I teased her.

"That's what keeps you doing it each day." She grinned. "To stretch it back out again."

"It would take weeks before I would dare to," I said, exaggerating my crippled movements as I climbed out of the shower.

"You'd be surprised," she said.

I wasn't certain what she meant and I turned to get a towel, then felt her fingers lightly on my shoulders and with one quick action she straightened my back, pushing through the tension so that the muscles moved much further than I was personally daring to move them. It was all so fast and unexpected, that I had to surrender totally to her grip, and it actually felt fine. "I see what you mean," I gasped.

She let go and I turned to kiss her, but my undersized skeleton snapped back, and the movement took much longer than I expected, so that before I could complete the turn, she had dropped her robe and darted into the shower, pulling the curtain playfully, but firmly, behind her.

"Perhaps I'll give you a back-rub later, if you're lucky," she offered. "I think I brought some oil." There was a rush of water and steam from the shower.

"Wow! Thanks." I rubbed the towel against my skin,

and my pores began to glow.

We finally woke Sarah and went out for food. It was already early afternoon and hot. My body was feeling better now, but the city still felt surreal, like it might twist or bend into something new without warning.

"It's too hot," Sarah complained for the tenth time. "Why couldn't we eat at the hotel?"

Zoe caught my eye, with a 'not again' expression. Minx was riding proudly on her shoulder.

"We'll find somewhere cool to eat," I repeated for the umpteenth time. "Lunch was already off at the hotel." She took my hand, and her gentle touch reminded me to make allowances for her age. "We'll find something nice soon," I assured her.

We stopped at the first cafe with air conditioning and an empty table in the window. "I want an orange juice," Sarah told the waiter, as soon as he put the menus on the table, "and a hamburger and chips."

He whipped out his note-pad.

"Can I get some mineral water and a foccacia," I said. "Smoked salmon?" he asked, and I nodded.

"I'll have one of those big bowls of coffee," Zoe said,

pointing at some on the next table. They were huge, with a thick layer of froth. She looked down at the menu for some moments. "I'll order food in a moment," she added.

"You should eat something," I told her.

"I just said I would," she said. "Don't father me."

"I just meant it in a caring..." but her look stopped me in mid sentence.

"He's terrible like that," Sarah agreed and the two women looked at one another in that infuriating female way.

After our food we found Trish in the Fringe office sitting behind a desk covered in piles if paper. "You're a day early," she protested.

"We drove straight through," I explained, wondering if the extra night's accommodation cost might be an issue. "We got here early this morning." Zoe put her arm around me. "This is Zoe. She's doing the chalk."

Trish smiled and leaned across the desk and shook her hand. Sarah pushed to the front and proffered her hand too, and Trish shook it solemnly. "I'm very pleased you could come," she told Sarah, who just nodded like this was the expected greeting.

Trish took a yellow card off her desk and offered it to her.

"What is it?" Sarah asked.

"It's a pass which will get you into any show in the Fringe."

"Free?" she asked, turning it over to explore the pin on the back. Trish nodded and Sarah's composed demeanor broke and she beamed and pinned it on her shirt.

Trish smiled and gave passes to Zoe and me.

"How's it going?" I asked.

"This is the first week, so the next few days will be crucial." Trish reflected for a moment and the flow of feelings across her face told more about the dramas of mounting and arts event than the words. "The main festival starts next week, so we have to make a mark this weekend, get some publicity and get people into the shows."

"We're here now," Sarah told her, as if that would really improve things.

Trish laughed. "Shall I show you the site?" she

asked. We nodded and she led us through the office and down some stairs, out into an open courtyard with tables and chairs grouped around several bars, and in the middle we discovered a pile of sand.

"Oh good," she seemed surprised. "It must have just been delivered." Sarah ran over and jumped in it. "Do you want to start today?" Trish asked.

"Sure," I responded spontaneously, thinking that would balance the extra night's accommodation cost.

"There don't seem to be many people around." Zoe was less enthusiastic. Minx poked his little head out of Zoe's pocket, and we laughed at his inquisitive expression.

"It gets busy in here in the evenings," Trish explained.

To one side of the sand stood a group of movable supports with a rope draped casually between them. Zoe strode over to them and set the barrier posts with decisive movements about the sand so that it was at the maximum distance away that the rope would allow. Then she stood and surveyed the space she had to work with. Minx scrambled up and out of her pocket, and scampered over the sand.

Sarah was hanging on my leg, and I shook her free. Trish looked at me. “Anything you need just let me know.”

I nodded. “Just leave us with it.”

“Okay, have fun.” She strode off .

I went and stood beside Zoe. "I'm sorry I just decided for us," I said, because it felt like she was resentful of not being consulted.

"It's fine," she said.

"You're allowed to, Dad," Sarah told me. "It's your game."

I looked at her and saw two trusting eyes. She was playing my game and would give me full control.

"It doesn't work like that," I told her gently. "It's all of our game now." I turned to Zoe. "I probably need to get my side of it under way first, anyway."

She shrugged and opened her shoulder bag to show me the box of chalks inside. "I came prepared," she said.

We set to work without any discussion, all of us doing our own thing, and I lost myself in the meditative playfulness of the activity. Sarah lost interest fairly early, and went to explore the courtyard with Minx, but my sand shapes seemed to flow naturally out through Zoe's colors into the surrounding space and we found again that casual creative partnership of our first meeting, one which demanded nothing of one another, and yet enhanced each other's work. This gave me a deep sense of fulfillment, and after all the drama of getting to this point, the sand work was pure joy, and within a couple of hours we had transformed the site into a mass of color and form.

As the evening came on, and the place slowly filled up around us, I sensed rather than heard the animated conversation and interest from the people around us.

"Let's eat," I finally said.

Zoe nodded, and stood up.

The place was packed now, and we stood side by side, surveying the results, then looked at one another. We had found a new level of intimacy, and she threw her arms around me and we kissed. Her lips were firm and delicate and I felt the energies stir between us. I realized that we had both been apprehensive that it might not work well together, and now the physical contact reaffirmed our relationship.

"No kissing," Sarah called over to us. She was sitting with a drink at the cafe nearby.

"Oh come on Sarah," I said. "I'm old enough to look after myself." She turned up her nose and pretended to ignore us. She had saved us a couple of seats however, and Minx was curled asleep on one. Zoe picked him up and we sat down. I ordered a salad and Zoe ordered a burger. I felt more satisfied than I had for days, the anticipation was finally over and the craft had begun again.

"Dad," Sarah drew me out of my thoughts. "Isn't that the man from Auckland?" She pointed to someone standing on the far side of the courtyard. The guy was observing, just as Adam had the first time we had met him on Bondi and, at first I thought this was what she meant, and then I realized it was indeed Adam. I stood and waved to attract his attention.

"This is the guy that took us to Auckland," I explained to Zoe as he made his way over.

"I see you've expanded," he said.

I nodded. "This is Zoe, she's the chalk."

"Good move."

She bowed her head in acknowledgment.

"Adam's from the Auckland Festival," I introduced him.

"Was," he responded.

We looked at him.

"Was from the Auckland Festival," he explained. "My contract wasn't renewed."

That seemed incredible... One week the man is running a successful festival, and the next he's out of a job. "What happened?" I couldn't get my head around it.

The salad and the burger arrived, and I watched Zoe eyeing her meal. Somehow it wasn't cool to enjoy it while Adam's drama was unfolding.

"It's karma," he said, shrugging it off.

His off-handedness released her to enjoy the food, and she started wolfing it down.

"But what sort of karma?" I asked, picking up a fork and playing with the red and green of the capsicum and the lettuce.

He bent his head in acknowledgement. "Indeed... The important question..."

"What's karma?" Sarah asked.

He pulled up a chair. He looked excited with the challenge of explaining it. "It's a bit like magic," he said. "We're each born with magic that we have to deal to, and we create more magic as we go, depending on how we play the game."

I smiled at Sarah's knowing expression and took a mouthful of the crisp juicy vegetables.

"And losing the job in Auckland?" Zoe prompted him.

"Was a piece of magic which I had to deal with, because of my past deeds," he explained "or as a motivation for me to learn something new, I don't know yet."

Territory

A man was hosing down the courtyard and the water sat in puddles and ran in streams on the uneven concrete floor. I sat up on a stool at one of the bars with Firefly, to avoid getting my feet wet as he came closer. He was half-asleep and the water was spraying up the walls, but, under Zoe's watchful eye, he was being careful of the sculpture.

"Would you like a lemonade?" someone behind the bar asked.

"I haven't got any money," I admitted.

"They're free with that," he said, motioning to my fringe pass.

Wow, I thought, free! I wanted to run and tell dad, but I was too cool, so I just nodded.

Minx was exploring the territory. The part of the courtyard which hadn't been washed, was still sticky with spilt beer, and every now and again he would leap in the air to free himself and then stop, to lick his paws. Firefly hopped down to play. She had no such problems, because she didn't really touch the ground when she walked. Then Minx discovered that the wet part of the floor wasn't sticky, but now he had to keep flicking his paws as he walked, to get the water off.

I giggled, because he looked so confused but also fascinated by all the new experiences. He got close to the man with the hose and wanted to play with the stream of water itself, but didn't realize how strong it was and was swept off his feet. He looked so little when his fur was wet. Firefly was also enjoying the water, dancing in the spray, leaping through the colors of the sun as the light played through the drops of water. Minx scrambled back to his feet, and shook himself. Then he saw Firefly, and there was a total stillness in his body for a moment before he leapt in the air after her.

I sipped my drink while I watched them play together. I was so busy watching, that the bubbles from the lemonade got into my nose and I had to swallow hard to stop from sneezing. Once they came too close to the sculpture and Minx skidded onto Zoe's chalk, but she just shooed him away.

The sculpture was looking good. Dad had created two wings of sand, stretching out from the center and, on top of them, I was making a castle with towers in the corners. The castle kind of stood out like a funny hat, perched on top of the wings, but somehow that made it look really good. Without me, they'd be nothing, I thought, and I sipped my drink. We should put a hat out, I thought, and see if we got any money. I was beginning to really like this new business. Going to festivals was way cool.

I did a once around of the courtyard when I had finished my lemonade. The man with the hose had finished, and the concrete was now clean and fresh again, but I discovered the stale smell of bear still hanging around the drains.

Dad and Zoe were into their work and didn't notice my arrival. "We should do more of this," I told them. "This is cool."

Dad slowly looked at me, and smiled. "We'll just have to see what happens," he said, in his funny way.

"Let's make it happen," I told him. Grown-ups always seemed to think things were more complicated than they really were.

"If we want to do more," Zoe suggested, "let's do this one as well as we can, and see where it leads."

It felt like she meant that I wasn't doing enough. "I wasn't talking to you," I told her. We eyed one another, and then I turned to dad. "We should put out a hat, and see if we get any money."

"That's what I've been thinking," Zoe said.

The last thing I wanted was her agreeing with me, so I just set to work on the castle.

"Watch out, you're on my stuff!" she called out a short while later, and I discovered I was standing on part of her chalk drawing.

I scampered back onto the sand pile. "Sorry," I mumbled, but I felt resentful that I had to make these allowances for her. There was only a small space in which I could stand now, and it was getting hot and I was beginning to feel tired. I sat on my haunches and watched her work. Dad was getting some drinks, and it was maybe the first time we had been working alone together.

"You don't feel comfortable with me?" she asked, looking up.

"Why should I?" I didn't want her getting personal.

"It would make it more fun," she suggested.

I grunted. "It would be more fun if you weren't here," I told her. Even to me, it sounded like a hateful thing to say, but it was my way of opening up. "And Firefly doesn't like you either." I don't know why I said it, and I looked down at the cracks in the concrete.

She took a breath. "Isn't your dad allowed girl friends?"

I found myself shaking my head before I could stop myself. "Sometimes," I acknowledged.

"When?"

I shrugged. I did like her. Maybe that's why I was pushing her away. I could see her sharing my life some time to come, if I wasn't very careful, but I was saved from replying by dad's return.

"Let's take a break this afternoon," he suggested. "And do some more this evening, when it cools down." A gust of wind pushed through the courtyard. The smell of beer from the drains was becoming stronger as the heat increased. "I hear the aquatic center is nice," he suggested. He was looking for Zoe's confirmation, rather than mine, and I resented this.

"Good idea," I told him, pushing in before her.

"Mind your manners," he told me. "There's more than just you to consider." It was then that I knew that I had lost the battle. Dad wading in with his 'bring you up properly' attitude, trampling all over our precious relationship as if it meant nothing, told me that the battle was lost.

So that night I let Zoe and Dad work without me, and I found a stool at the corner of the bar and sat reading.

"Are you supervising tonight?" Someone burst in on my thoughts, and I discovered Adam standing beside me.

I nodded. He went to sit down on the stool beside me and stopped. "Firefly's sitting here?" he asked.

I nodded. "Can't you see her?"

He shook his head. "I thought she was invisible."

"Only to most people."

He sat down in another chair.

"I'm surprised someone with your magic can't see her," I told him.

"Maybe I can learn to," he said. He had a twinkle in his eye, but I couldn't tell if he was excited with the idea, or making fun of me.

"Have you seen Minx?" Zoe was suddenly standing beside us sounding worried.

I felt a little smile inside. God was on my side. Maybe a little of it showed however, for she looked at me as if I had done something with the kitten. "I... I haven't seen him," I stammered.

"Hasn't been here," Adam agreed.

Zoe's look stayed for a moment longer, and then she turned to go.

I poked my tongue after her.

"Are you two having a thing?" Adam asked.

I shrugged, and determined to change the subject. "I saw what you were talking about in the video game today," I told him. He looked puzzled. "You been to the aquatic center?" I asked.

He shook his head.

"It's huge, with pools and waterfalls and slides," I put my book down. "I was there and I found some kids to play with." He nodded. He seemed to be able to listen in a way, which was unusual for a big person. "One of the guys had some money and I got a couple of goes with him on the video games. Boy it was fun! You had to get round the obstacles, and find the treasure."

He smiled, not fully understanding.

"That's like that karma thing," I explained. "The second time I chose a different way to go, and it worked better.

He nodded. "However in life we can't go back and take a different way, we have to live with our choices."

"Sometimes you can do it again a different way," I told him, because sometimes you can.

"Sometimes," he agreed, smiling and tousling my hair. "That's how we learn. Everything we do, gives us the best lessons for our growth, if we let it."

I liked his way of looking at things.

"I hear there is a good magic show starting in a few minutes," he said. "Do you want to come?"

I sat up. "How much does it cost?"

He motioned to my pass. "I think you can get in free with that." He was also wearing one, but his was a different color.

"Let's go," I said, jumping up.

He smiled. "We better ask your dad."

I ran across to tell him. Zoe had found Minx again and was playing with him with a piece of string. He was jumping for it and she was lifting it out of reach. "I'm going to a magic show with Adam," I announced.

Dad kissed me. "Have fun," he said. At that moment, I forgave him for everything. It wasn't his fault, after all, and I loved him, and cuddled against him.

Inside the theater, the lights dimmed, and a spotlight came up on the magician. He produced a ball from his mouth. He showed it to us, and then put it in his pocket, and then another appeared.

At first, I thought he had a big mouth, but when he did it ten times, I couldn't work out how it was happening.

"How does he do it?" I whispered to Firefly. She was sitting on my lap entranced, and made no reply. So I looked at Adam, but he was also lost in the performance, smiling like a big boy, and I nudged him and giggled, like I imagined I would if I had a kid brother.

Doing Pretty Well

"Do you see that man doing the sand sculptures?" a man asked a woman. "He senses the judgment of destiny, and so he is forever playing, putting off that moment when he must take responsibility for really making his mark on the world."

The woman first observed the convivial feeling in the courtyard and then the cluster of people around the sculpture itself.

Finally she looked at her friend leaning against the wall, a beer in his hand, and his stomach stretching along the bar, and she also sensed the judgment of destiny.

"I think he's doing pretty well," she tried to awaken her friend.

Power of Magic

Adam ordered a late breakfast in the Fringe courtyard and the sand sculptors arrived, with the kitten bounding along behind, as his plate of fried eggs and mushrooms was placed on the table.

"Hi guys." He smiled at them, saving a special gleam for Sarah. "You want to sit down?" She sat without hesitation, she was cuddling a teddy bear.

Zoe shook her head. "The television's coming today," she said.

He pursed his lips and blew through them to express how suitably impressed he was. "You guy's handle the media superbly."

"It happens by accident," Sax told him, walking around the sculpture, surveying it in the morning light.

"I think there's a lesson there," Adam suggested.

"I know," Sax agreed. "Have we talked about this?"

Adam shook his head. Minx leapt up into his lap and then lifted up his nose to explore the smells from the table. "That's my food," he warned the kitten. The little face looked up at him, uncertain.

Sarah grinned.

Unable to resist, Minx put his front paws on the table, and brought his nose in closer, to explore the individual smells from the plate. Adam tapped him lightly on the nose before he could touch the food, and he retreated back into his lap, and curled up.

"He likes you," Zoe said.

"We'll see if he likes me as much when this is finished," Adam said, devoting himself to his food.

"Do some magic," Sarah told him.

"I'm eating."

"When you've finished?"

"We'll see." The mushrooms were beautifully done, and he savored the taste. “It was good last night huh?”

Sarah’s thumb was back in her mouth, and she just nodded as she watched her dad maneuver himself across part of the chalk and flicked water onto a crumbling section of the wing.

Suddenly she leapt up, ran over the chalk and thrust her bear into his arms. "I've got to go to the toilet," she explained, as she hopped dramatically from foot to foot, and then ran off.

He stood with the precious toy, totally interrupted in his own process, and exchanged glances with Zoe.

Adam wondered why Sarah hadn't just left the bear with him, but he guessed that only her dad could be entrusted with it.

Sax looked for somewhere to put it that wasn't covered in sand or chalk and, finding nowhere, nestled it right on the top of the sand pile before returning to work.

Adam cleaned up the last of the food, and was just finishing as Sarah ran back into the courtyard, stopping when she saw that her father was not still holding the bear. She stormed over to him. It looked like a deliberate performance. "Where's teddy?" she demanded.

The tone of her voice triggered frustration in her father. "Why should I look after your stuff," he demanded in return. "And watch out for Zoe's chalk."

They glared at one another, and the miscommunication between them touched Adam. Sarah had entrusted her toy to her father, and when that trust was betrayed she took it as a personal rejection. She poked her tongue at him and flounced back to the table. Adam pointed out the bear, nestled in pride of place against her castle wall on the crown of the sculpture, and she looked relieved, but was now too angry to go and get it.

"Are you going to do some magic now?" she demanded, seeing his empty plate. The way she said it, he didn't want to. He hadn't seen this side of her before, and he shook his head. She stood and flounced off.

He pushed the plate away, opened the paper, and discovered a photo of the sand sculpture. 'Festival discovery captivates the fringe,' ran the caption followed by a brief article, which mentioned their discovery at the Auckland Festival.

Zoe sat down. "I need a coffee," she said, "before I can get into it today." She placed a bowl on the table in front of her. He showed her the photo and she grinned. "I've never been in the paper before." The picture was taken from a low angle so that the chalk work was prominent and the sand rose out of it, with a background of animated audience faces.

"I love what you bring to the sand sculpture," he told her.

"Thanks."

"It becomes more like a three dimensional mandala."

She smiled. "Thanks."

"You and Sax have an intuitive contact."

"We don't talk about what we're going to do," she agreed, "we just do it."

He nodded. "I guess that comes from working together."

"This is the first time."

"But when you know someone well, you get to understand them."

"We just met."

"Wow!" He grinned. "You've settled into the family quickly."

A sound like a choke escaped her mouth, and then she threw back her head and laughed.

"No?" he asked.

She shook her head. "I don't think I'm much of a family person." She sipped her coffee, cradling the bowl in both hands.

Sarah appeared, looking a little more humble and circled around the table, to come to rest behind his chair. He felt her standing there and guessed from Zoe's expression that she was playing distraction games.

"What are you doing after this?" Zoe asked, fixing her gaze on Adam.

"I'll find something," he assured her. A thought occurred to him, and he grinned. "Maybe I should manage you guys. You look very successful."

They laughed.

"Do you think Adam should manage us," Zoe asked Sarah, inviting her out from behind the chair.

"And you could magic up festivals for us to work at," she said, joining them at the table. Her belief touched him. He took out the cards and her eyes widened. He shuffled, then checked the bottom card. It was the queen of spades. He manipulated it into the middle of the deck, and fanned it face down in front of her.

"Take any card," he told her, taking care that the card he wanted her to take was right in front and poking slightly further out, just as she was ready to take one. She took the card he was offering.

"Look at it," he told her. "I'm going to read your mind." She grinned, and closed her eyes. He noticed the attention of people around them and caught the eye of one old woman at the next table, and they shared an enjoyment of Sarah's faith.

"Look at the card," he told her again. She opened her eyes and stared at it. He took some moments to concentrate and increase the dramatic tension. "I think you've got a black card," he told her.

She looked at him blankly, like she wasn't supposed to give away any clues.

"Is it a black one?" he asked. She nodded. "It's a high card," he went on, "a picture card... I think it's a queen?" She grinned, and there was a look of wonder on her face. "The queen of spades," he said, and she nodded.

He motioned her to show the small circle of onlookers the card, and enjoyed the suspension of disbelief evident in the grins and frowns. This was magic abroad in the world. People always associated magic with the trick itself, but it was rather the bending of reality so as to accept incongruous events.

The old woman at the next table had been trying to work it out. She motioned to him to do it for her and, as he turned his chair towards her, the circle of onlookers drew closer.

He sat doing card magic until well into the heat of the afternoon, and throughout that time there was a constant audience around the table. Where yesterday, he recalled that the courtyard had been fairly empty during the heat of the day, today it was alive with activity. He lost all sense of time in the constant interaction with people and enjoyed the sensation that each moment was valid of itself. Drinks and food appeared at the table when ever he needed something, provided first by members of the audience and later by the Fringe when it was realized what an attraction he was providing.

A television camera pushed through the spectators at one point, to capture a close-up of the magic. Adam felt exposed, and strangely disempowered by the intrusion of the technology. Magic happens in the imagination, he thought, and they haven't developed cameras to capture that yet. The camera panned up to his face, and a microphone appeared in front of him.

"Are you performing in the Fringe?" he was asked.

He shook his head.

"So you're just a member of the public who has come down to the Fringe to practice your card tricks?"

Adam felt challenged by this in several ways, and was initially uncertain how to respond. "I think one of the big benefits of a Fringe Festival," he chose his words deliberately, "is that it does encourage creativity in the community." He felt satisfied with that, and savored the next challenge for a moment. "I also love the look of wonder on people's faces when they can't explain reality, and I think somewhere in there lives a real magic, a sense of magic which connects us with the world in different ways to those we can see everyday."

In the end, he worked until early evening, when he began to feel exhausted, and then he went back to the hotel to rest. He lay down on the bed. He felt cleansed by the wash of interactions and experienced a quiet presence in his body, a sensation which normally followed meditation, before falling into a sound sleep in his clothes.

Repeated Lessons

Sax and Sarah were standing beside a pool of water at a pedestrian crossing and a car cut the corner too closely, spraying them lightly with water. They burst into laughter from the shock.

"Did you see that?" Sax exclaimed. "That car just sprayed us with water!"

Sarah was moving away as her father spoke. Out of the corner of her eye, she saw a bus approaching.

Sax brushed the water off his clothes. "I can't believe that," he said, unable to let go of his surprise. The next moment the bus cut even closer than the car, and a big splash of water drenched him, while Sarah managed to jump out of the way.

He looked at her, the water dripping off him, and she grinned. "Do you believe it now?" she asked.

Dangerous Intimacy

Inspiration was like energy, Zoe thought, you could recharge it simply by absorbing art. They had taken the afternoon off, and she had spent the time cruising the galleries and seen some really interesting stuff. It was almost six when she got back to the hotel, and discovered Sax and Sarah in front of the television in their room.

"Did you have a good time?" Sax asked. He was still holding resentment from her rejection of his suggestion for the afternoon, she realized, and she couldn't even remember what it had been.

"Sometimes I need some space," she told him. "We don't need to spent every minute together."

"It's coming on! It's coming on!" Sarah was bouncing with excitement as the news started.

Zoe felt suddenly apprehensive as she remembered

how she had burbled on before the camera, and now she wondered what she had said.

Sax passed her the paper. "It's this mornings.. We made page three. That's why it was so much buzzier down there today."

"I know," she told him, cuffing him lightly over the head as she passed it back. She was beginning to see the nobbly bits in him, the annoying traits, which she would rather overlook. It was always like this in her relationships after a while, and she realized she had been mulling this over in her subconscious during the day. Minx was curled on the bed, and she sat beside him and fondled his ears.

"*The Fringe Festival is always looking for new and innovative art,*" the news-reader announced, "*and this year they have found a new sculptural group from Sydney using a novel yet familiar medium.*" The visual cut to Zoe working with the chalk, and panning over the sand to where Sax was working. It looked good, she thought, and she breathed easier. Then the camera cut to a close up on her, and she felt her heart leap into her throat.

"*Yes, it could be more lucrative to work in a more*

permanent medium," she heard herself repeat the interviewer's question, *"but there's something beautiful about the short life span of this work. It's part of its artistic nature. You have to appreciate it while it's here. And I think we see a bit of our own lives reflected in that symbolically... I think we see a reminder to enjoy life while we can."*

The item moved on to other aspects of the Fringe, and the others looked at her, as if she'd taken the only slice of cake. "We'll have to make you the official spokesperson," Sax said dryly.

"They didn't even show me," Sarah complained.

"You weren't really doing it today," Zoe told her. She felt elated that she had used her moment of fame to say something meaningful. The news item flicked back to the courtyard, with a shot of Adam doing magic. "I love the look of wonder on people's faces when they can't explain reality," he said, "and I think that somewhere in there lives a real magic, a sense of magic which connects us with the world in different ways to those we can see everyday."

Sarah jumped up and down. "It's Adam."

"And that perhaps sums up the Fringe," the announcer ended brightly.

Sax switched it off. "Okay, back to work," he said in his gruff organizing voice, but he paused to kiss Zoe and she found his lips were sensitive and loving, and she sensed his appreciation and a little jealousy in his touch. "I never know what to say," he confided.

It was funny, she realized, but the more he tried to connect with her when she was in this mood, the more she wanted to push him away.

The courtyard was raging again that night and, as she sat rubbing part of the chalk image with a rag to blur the color textures, she found her attention wandering. She was on cloud nine from the trance of seeing herself on the television and couldn't really focus on the detail of the work in front of her.

She decided to get a coffee, and had started threading her way across the courtyard, when suddenly a strange guy grabbed her by the hand. "I think you guys are doing great stuff," he said, beaming as if they were old friends.

He was vaguely familiar, but she couldn't place him.

"Thanks," she mumbled, feeling embarrassed that he was holding her hand.

"I just wanted you to know," he said, letting go.

"Thanks," she said again. As she walked away she recalled he had been the person at the registration desk, when they first arrived at the Fringe. Funny that he should feel that familiar with her, she thought.

Coffee in hand, she stood looking at their work. It was like an island in a sea of intoxicated life. She became aware of Trish and Sax talking heatedly on the other side of the sand, and although she couldn't hear what they were saying, their body-language drew her over to find out.

"You really undermined my efforts to extend your season," Trish told her as she joined them. Her tone was sharp and Zoe was startled. She took a few moments connecting with what Trish might mean and so she didn't respond immediately.

"I was negotiating funds for an extension," Trish fumed.

Zoe shrugged, still not understanding the link with her, or the strong emotion.

"We wouldn't have extended anyway," Sax told Trish. "I made an exception in Auckland, because we got rained out one day..." He let the sentence trail off, implying that there were many other reasons.

Zoe clicked that her television comments had triggered this reaction.

"That's a shame," Trish said. "I was going to offer you a lucrative deal."

Sax grinned and motioned to their hat, which was full of coins. Zoe found this was a brave move in the circumstances and her intuition was proven right.

"You see," Trish exclaimed, "already you're getting a better deal than most participants, because we're covering your costs, and you're taking the profit!"

Sax shrugged. "That was our deal."

Trish looked at him in exasperation.

"What was it Christo said?" Sax asked, "when the German government wanted to extend the wrapping of the Richtstag for a third week, after delaying it for over thirty years?"

"We are like Bedouins pitching out tents in the sand," Zoe paraphrased his words. "There comes a time to move on." She liked the sentiment of the statement, and she liked the fact that Sax also connected with it. She took his hand and they renewed their bond through the touch.

"So you won't extend it?" Trish demanded.

They nodded together.

Trish took stock for a moment. "Maybe I've come on too strong about this," she admitted, "but it's just that I'm bending over backwards for you guys." The energy in the courtyard surged as people came out from one of the venues. "What about doing a sculpture in a suburban shopping center for a couple of days?"

Zoe shook her head, and looked at Sax for support, and to her horror found him nodding. They held one another's gaze and their fingers reaffirmed their love while their eyes sought some consensus.

He pursed his lips. "Why not?"

"In a suburban shopping center?" she reminded him.

"What sort of deal?" he asked Trish.

"Same as here," she said. "We have extra funding to encourage community projects in the outlying suburbs.

He looked at Zoe and, although she didn't want to do it, she shrugged.

"I'll take that as a maybe," Trish said. "We can talk more tomorrow."

She left them holding hands and contemplating the future. Zoe felt very close to Sax, closer than maybe any of her relationships, and she realized this made her feel vulnerable and powerless, feelings which she hated. She was experiencing a tidal pull away from the relationship as it deepened, she realized.

"She just seemed so desperate," Sax explained his response.

"That was her way of getting us to agree."

"Weird how emotional she was."

She nodded.

"Who was that guy holding your hand earlier?"

She blushed. "I don't know. That was weird too. He said he wanted to thank us."

"It's being media celebrities."

She nodded.

They turned to each other and their lips met and, despite her hesitations and the very public surroundings, it seemed easy to plunge in deeper when she felt the risk rewarded by the passion.

Understanding & Illusion

Sarah was in a hurry and the train was late.

Suddenly she lashed out and hit the back of the seat beside her and the release of energy made her feel better.

"If it doesn't come in the next minute, you'll get another," she hissed at the seat.

Sure enough when no train arrived, she hit it again. The loud noise it made brought her satisfaction.

"Don't make me do it a third time," she told it.

Some of the people around her were looking strangely at her, but she was also doing it for their benefit, so she was prepared to ignore their stares and punish the seat a third time, but of course she didn't need to, because just then the train arrived.

Coming to Terms

I got up early and went down to the breakfast room of the hotel. It was going to be a scorcher of a day, and already the window panels onto the street had been removed to allow for maximum flow of air.

I ordered a tea and chose a table, which was right on the pavement and so provided a ring-side seat on the passing pedestrians.

I hadn't slept well, which was a bad sign, and I was searching for the reason. Something was happening with Zoe that I didn't understand, and I spent some time chewing this over without much result.

I decided that I was probably just projecting my own insecurities onto her, and I let my thoughts get carried away with the passing flow of people.

Some time later she sat down at the table.

"Where's Sarah?" I asked.

"She's watching the box... She'll be okay."

"She might miss breakfast."

"No chance."

I nodded. Across the road two men in suits stepped out of a doorway, a bible in each of their right hands. They lifted their feet, one after the other, and brushed their free hand over the soles of their shoes. "Look, they brush away the bad energy when they are rejected," I pointed out.

She looked at them.

"When people don't want to hear the word of God." As we considered this, a child hopped past, carefully avoiding the cracks in the paving stones. "It's like we build our beliefs to explain the chaotic experience of being alive." I was thinking out loud.

"Maybe." she shrugged. "Or maybe there is a truth that exists beyond all of the illusions that we create for ourselves." It was my turn to shrug. It never seemed that simple to me. We looked at one another. "This is the last day," she reminded me.

We had grown very close, very quickly. "But we're going to the suburb?" I quickly sought security in the plan and realized how much I wanted it all to keep going.

She grimaced. "I guess."

"Can it keep being so beautiful?"

She smiled. "Time will tell."

I nodded, but sensed something else behind her reluctance and allowed space for her to reveal it.

"It's been a bit intense," she finally said.

"What?"

"With you."

"How do you mean?" My fears were being manifest right before my eyes, as usual.

"Just suddenly into my life like this."

"That's what's beautiful."

"And scary."

"Why?"

"Because I lose control."

"That's what's beautiful," I repeated.

She slapped me playfully on the shoulder, and the physicality reassured me.

"Maybe we should have a holiday," I suggested. "Why don't we take some time driving back to

Sydney?" She suggested.

"Great idea!" I agreed, although I immediately realized it would mean more time out of school for Sarah.

"Maybe the Fringe will pay for the car."

I shrugged. I didn't want to ask. "Why don't you see if they will?"

She looked at me. Until now I had done all the organizing. "Okay, I will," she agreed.

I took some time in the afternoon taking photos of the sculpture. Sarah had found her game boy, and was propped up on one of the courtyard tables, her attention transfixed by the tiny screen.

I sat down beside her to change my film.

"Can you not move the table like that?" she asked, without even glancing at me.

Her tone annoyed me, however before I could respond Zoe bounded up, all excited. She took a piece of paper out of her pocket and waved it, then placed it on the table. It was a hire car chit, made out for five days.

"Looks good!" I congratulated her.

Sarah looked up from the screen long enough to

realize that she didn't understand what was going on, and she paused her game and looked at me. "We're going to take a few days driving back," I explained, "have a holiday."

"Thanks for asking me," she responded.

We looked at one another. I felt my defensiveness rising again at her accusing tone. "You've been a bit buried in the appliances today," I told her. She poked out her tongue and then duly buried her attention back in the game. The heat was aggravating our mood, I decided.

Zoe took out another chit for hundred dollars. "That's the petrol costs," she explained. "And we stay where we are for the next couple of days while we do the suburb."

"That's perfect!" I agreed.

I reached out and rubbed my hand up her back, and we leaned against one another and allowed our energies to merge. In the heat of the afternoon the courtyard was totally deserted. "There's a yoga class I think I might check out," Zoe suggested.

"I want to go back to the hotel!" Sarah protested.

"Why?" I asked.

"It's air-conditioned!"

It made sense. "We can have an afternoon nap," I suggested. She half nodded. That wasn't quite her idea, I sensed, but she was prepared to go along with it to get out of the heat. I leaned towards Zoe and we kissed. "See you later," I told her.

Sarah would have been happy watching television or playing video games all day, because she sat straight back down in front of the box when we got to the hotel. I tried to sleep, and then gave up and lay thinking.

I wondered if we'd made the right decision. The suburbs would be a very different setting for the work, and it might not be easy.

I drifted into a half dream in which I saw us transforming the bland atmosphere of a shopping center into a cultural event which surprised and enlivened the community. In my imagination it became so popular that the local mayor made a special visit to present us with awards, and the media were on hand to capture the moment for history.

Back in the hotel room the flicker of the light on

Sarah's face was an eerie blue color which gave the impression that she was mesmerized and controlled by the technology. Perhaps Zoe had been right about her schooling, I thought, and then I pushed that idea away. The sound of the television kept gnawing away at my sense of peace however, until at the end of one of the cartoons, I got up and turned it off.

"Hey, why'd you do that?" Sarah demanded.

"That's enough for now," I told her. "You've had too much already." I sat back on the bed.

"Why?"

"It makes you silly."

"I'm not being silly."

"Too much, makes you silly."

"But I haven't had too much!"

"I have." I wanted to put an end to the debate. "Anyway, I want to talk with you."

"What about?"

"The next couple of days."

"What about it?"

"Maybe it's better that we get you back to school."

"Don't do the suburb?" she asked, sounding out my

intentions.

"Zoe and I can do it, and you can fly back."

Her attitude hardened. "Dad, this is the coolest, why would I worry about school?"

"But you haven't really been into it here."

"What do you mean?'

I realized she thought that by watching television in the hotel room she was being really into it. Maybe she was right, but I wasn't in the mood to let it rest. "Well, in Auckland you did half the work, but here you've been just fiddling around really."

"Without my castle that thing would look like shit," she told me, offended by my dismissive attitude to her work. "And anyway, you've got someone else doing half of it this time!"

I was taken aback by the strength of her reaction.

"You just want to send me away so you can have a couple of days with her and without me," she said.

"I wasn't thinking that at all," I protested. She had me on the defensive immediately.

"Which is why I have to stay!"

"It's not about that, it's about what's right for you."

"Is that what you were thinking about when you decided to take an extra few days holiday?"

"No," I admitted. "But it's what I'm thinking about now."

"When you want to have that holiday without me."

"No. It's not like that."

"You're stuck with me, dad."

I grinned. "I'm glad. Just so long as you can look after yourself."

"You're the one that needs looking after." She jumped on me and pushed me backwards onto the bed. "That's why it's good that I'm here."

I pulled her into a cuddle, and she struggled dutifully for a brief moment, before we relaxed in one another's arms. It made no sense to me as usual, but I was getting used to that.

It was a celebration that night in the courtyard. People kept coming up and congratulating us, and Sarah was of course particularly enjoying the popularity. Someone gave Zoe a bottle of Champagne, but I felt strangely distant to the hubbub and I left it to her. It had been a special time and I was conscious of it ending.

At one point, when Sarah was playing hide and seek with Firefly around my legs, Trish appeared on a stage in a corner of the courtyard and tapped the microphone.

"Ladies and Gentlemen!" Her voice boomed commandingly though the space and yet the attention of the crowd was slow in coming. Everyone was high on art and alcohol, and she did a sort of comic dance to hold the focus while the noise settled. She seemed a little drunk, but people appreciated it, and her effort received a big applause.

"Now that I have your attention," she said, "I want to thank the sand sculptors who have been working here over the past few days, and who have done so much to kick the fringe off this year."

There was more applause, and the noise reverberated in the confined space, stirring strong emotions inside me.

I caught Zoe's eye and saw similar emotions in her and we threw our arms around one another and hugged. Her touch helped, but I was a little dizzy. Sarah tightened her grip on my leg, and I reached around and pulled her into the cuddle. She burrowed in between us.

We separated and I stood unsteadily. Sarah returned to her game with my leg, but I had to push her away to get some space. Trish went on to other announcements and then Adam appeared beside Zoe.

"Congratulations!" he said.

Zoe spontaneously kissed him on the cheek, however to me it all happened in slow motion, and I was left with an awkward feeling from the display of affection. "Did you see your bit on the news?" she asked him.

He smiled. "It actually made some sense." His tone of wonder was so child-like, that we laughed.

"Like some wine?" she asked.

"Yes thanks," he responded. She poured a glass for him. "To your continued success," he toasted us, and they clinked glasses.

"We were thinking that Adam could manage us," Sarah suddenly said. I looked at her. The comment had come out of nowhere and yet she had a sly gr in, like she knew she was poking a tender spot.

I looked at Adam. He also grinned. "We were kidding

around."

"I think it's a very good idea," Zoe said.

I had a sense of vertigo, a feeling that things were moving about me, without me knowing what was happening. I was at one of those nodal points, where everything was about to change. All I had to do was let it happen and it would all be beautiful, but, as I saw Zoe and Adam both grinning at me, I had a deep knowledge that my karmic baggage wasn't going to let it be that easy.

"We're in the suburbs tomorrow," I said, stalling for time, but on hearing myself, I knew my emotions were evident.

There was a moment where the wash of noise about us seemed to swell and we each contemplated tomorrow. "Perhaps I'll come out with you for the day," he suggested.

"Yea!" Sarah exclaimed. "Come, come!"

"I'd like that," Zoe encouraged him. "If nothing else, it would relieve the claustrophobia of the family a little." She looked at me, and there was a hint of apology in her contact, which only made the effect of the comment sharper.

I suddenly felt very tired, and I noticed Sarah was almost hanging from my leg. "I think we'll go back to the hotel," I announced, and I felt proud of myself for making that choice.

I looked down at Sarah, and saw her evaluating Zoe's glass of wine, which was still half full. Then she caught my gaze. "Yes let's, I'm so tired," she said. She overplayed it, and there was an awkward moment where I had committed myself to a course of action but nothing was happening, and I looked at Zoe and felt the separation that is always there between two individuals.

"I'm going to hang out here a little," she answered my unarticulated question. "I'll see you back there."

Her eyes asked me to trust her and, with the insight that I could do nothing else, and the will of the warrior, I took Sarah back to the hotel. I felt the fear of the unknown in the process, but also happy with myself for my strength.

Zoe crept into bed with me later that night, and I felt her cold feet and hands, and her lips on my neck. My dreams till then had left me tossing and turning and

I welcomed the comfort of her soft touch as she cuddled against me. I felt our energies melt together and then fell directly into a deep sleep.

Wisdom Of The Stream

A pool spoke to the stream that flowed through it, and said: "You, who travel far and pass by much in the world, can you not find a way to stop the wind, for it comes from around that hill, and stirs up my delicate surface?"

"No," responded the stream. "There is no known way of stopping the wind."

"But can you not undertake a research?" the pool begged. "Or promote some investigation so that we can uncover this information?"

"All this effort would be wasted," the stream responded. "For the wind will always blow where she pleases."

However as time passed and the wind continued to dance with the pool, the stream suddenly floated up from within the stream.

"I do have a suggestion," it said to the pool one day, and the pool rippled with excitement. "The land on the shore, where the wind comes round the mountain, is owned by a man with a love of nature, who builds great gardens on my banks. If he could look into your tranquil surface, and if a sudden gust was to trouble that surface, perhaps he would be motivated to plant a wind-break of trees to provide some shelter."

The pool bubbled with excitement. "How will we ask the man?" it asked the stream.

"Unfortunately," responded the stream, "there is no known way of asking the man."

Soul Food

"Any luck?" Zoe asked, as she met Sax and Adam back at the only cafe in the Shopping Center.

"I made sure they knew what a waste of our time it was for us to sit around here, doing nothing!" Sax told her.

"A fat lot of good that does," she said, recognizing, but surrendering to, her instinct to push him away to protect herself.

He looked at her, helpless to know what he should do. The sand had not arrived, and without it there wasn't much they could do. Sarah stopped behind his chair and draped her arms protectively around his neck.

"It sounds like you could have been a bit more diplomatic," Adam agreed.

"Thanks for your opinion!" Sax fired back at him.

"Boys, boys!" Zoe tried to calm things. The tedium of

the morning was getting to them all. "So what's going to happen now?"

"I don't know," Sax admitted. He seemed so helpless.

"I knew this would happen," she told him. She was beginning to feel dangerously vulnerable to the successes or failures in his life. "That's why I didn't want to do it."

"Well, you haven't been much help!" he protested.

The hair on her neck bristled.

"There's no point in taking this out on one another," Adam reminded them.

"I'm glad someone here has a cool head," she said.

"Why don't you do something then?" Sax told Adam.

Adam turned sharply at his tone, then reflected for a moment. "Okay," he said. "I'll try." He stood and walked towards the management office.

Zoe released her frustration by pounding around the building, making it her territory like an animal. There wasn't much to it really, just a big concrete box, filled with plastic, glass and florescent lights. Her head was pounding from the after-effects of the champagne last night, and the movement helped to clear the cobwebs.

Minx bounded along beside her, alternately stalking at her heels and sliding helplessly on the polished tiles, and Sarah half-tagged along behind them, demonstrating her boredom every now and again with a loud sigh or an irreverent kick of some fixture, like a seat or a pot plant.

Zoe found her disrespect annoying and, in an attempt to smooth the process of their art in this alien space, she started blessing the fixtures instead, particularly the plants. She didn't make a big deal of it, simply pausing beside them momentarily and appreciating their existence. Soon however she noticed that Sarah had started watching more intently and she played up to this, adding some devout gestures to her movements.

"You did that one already," Sarah told her, as she paused beside one particularly beautiful palm for the second or third time. The gleam in the girl's eye told of her excitement at a big person entering into the magical realm in this way and Zoe felt a bond beginning to develop between them.

Arriving back at the café she found Sax sitting by himself, lost in contemplation and she touched him on the hand to bridge the gulf between them. Their fingers at first gently caressed, and then found a warm clasp.

"Let's do some yoga while we wait," she suggested.

"I don't really feel for it."

"All the more reason."

"I'm still sore from yesterday," he protested.

"That's the best time."

Minx jumped up onto the table and she fondled him behind the ears with her free hand. Sarah crept up behind her father and pounced on him, then leaned forward to rub her face in the kitten's fur as if nothing had happened. Minx turned his face to her, and they touched noses.

"Can you look after him while we do yoga?" Zoe asked, and Sarah scooped the kitten into her arms without a moment's hesitation.

Zoe grinned at Sax and he rolled his eyes to the ceiling in response. She stood. They were still holding hands and she pulled him to his feet and dragged him outside.

Afterwards they found Adam beside a pile of sand, at the back entrance to the shopping center. He had a wheelbarrow and was holding a shovel, and Minx sat grooming himself on top of the sand, as befits the 'King of the castle'.

"This was the only place that the truck could access," Adam explained, "because of the weight."

At the door to a nearby cake shop a large woman with a faded floral apron gazed at the sand and shook her head.

Zoe had to laugh. It reminded her of Don Quiote's valiant attempts to deal to the chaos of his perceptions. Her fingers sought Sax's, and she drew comfort from their touch. She sensed that had they not done the yoga, their relationship may have slowly dissolved, but the peaceful intimacy she felt between them now brought with it a renewal of faith.

Sarah came running around the corner of the building and jumped into the sand, which sent Minx flying.

"We have to move it ourselves," Adam said,

motioning to the wheelbarrow with his shovel.

Even Sax laughed.

"You guys seem much happier!" Adam was relieved at their reactions.

Zoe felt good, but she felt better once they got to work. The men loaded the wheelbarrow, and she and Sarah took turns at wheeling it into the shopping mall and dumping it. At first they started with a pile in the middle of the open court, but when one of Sarah's loads ended up half way down the mall, they left it there, because it was the easiest thing to do. However as Zoe wheeled her next few loads past Sarah's mound, she liked its placement in the space, and she spontaneously added another load to it, and stood for a moment, looking at what it was doing to the mall. She got lost in the contemplation and Sarah finally came to see what was happening.

"Did you drop it?"

"No, I think we should have more here."

"More here?"

They looked at one another and Zoe saw that gleam of excitement again in Sarah's eyes. "We could put them all over," she suggested, looking around the polished concrete.

"Yeah," Zoe said, catching the excitement.

"Better ask dad." Sarah suddenly wanted to play it safe.

"Do you think so?" Zoe asked.

They looked at one another for a moment and then Sarah shook her head. Zoe grinned. There was a rebel in both of them, and they started placing their loads randomly throughout the central court area.

Zoe let Sarah do the last few, while she started working with the chalk, using large strokes to place the mounds in some context, before Adam and Sax saw them.

She expected some controversy, however their reactions were not what she expected, for it was Adam, not Sax who was upset.

"You're just going to cause trouble!" Adam warned, a look of shock on his face.

Zoe shrugged. "It's good to be a little controversial."

Sax just stood beside Adam grinning.

Adam shook his head. "You've really disappointed

me."

"I'm sorry?" she asked. Her relationship with him was going through an about turn. The last thing she needed was more expectations from him.

"You're just making it harder for us," Adam told her.

"Fuck off," she told him. "Who's us, white man?"

He looked at her, speechless for some moments and then simply walked away. Minx was digging in one of the mounds, spraying sand behind him into the path of shoppers who scrambled to get out of the way.

Sarah couldn't hide a grin. "Come on guys," she told them, "we'll never get it done."

The rest of the afternoon did feel like an obstacle course, dealing with confused shoppers and annoyed shopkeepers, but Zoe enjoyed the challenge of keeping herself focused on the work. She liked it when art provoked a response, and the more people looked askance at them, the more she felt herself rising to the occasion.

Sarah was really going for it with the sand, all hint of castles abandoned under the demands of the scale of work, and after a while Sax left her to it and fetched his instrument from the car.

The sound of the saxophone filled the concrete box of the building, softening the edges to provide a friendlier context for their art, and the day finally settled into place for Zoe as she abandoned herself to the creativity.

Some time later she became aware of the polished shoes of a security guard standing beside her, and then the sound gentle gongs through a sound system.

“Attention shoppers,” the sound system politely requested, “this center will be closing in ten minutes. Please finalize your purchases and make your way to the exits.”

Zoe felt like they only just got going, and she bent to finish what she was working on, and also to avoid looking from the shoes, up the legs, to the authority standing beside her.

The guard moved on, to inspect the other’s work and she watched him out of the corner of her eye. His body was tense, under the provocation of this incomprehensible activity.

Adam met them at the entrance in the hire car. The

women and the kitten bundled into the back and Sax got in beside Adam.

Adam had been absent since their earlier encounter, and now he seemed detached, but Zoe sensed that there was stuff to resolve between them.

As they drove back into town however, she felt satisfied that she had made the work her own, in very difficult circumstances. Minx was curled in her lap, and Sarah lay with her head resting on Zoe's thigh, her face buried in the fluffy ball of the kitten.

Zoe scratched Minx behind the ears until he started purring. She could feel Sarah's small body slowly relax as she fell asleep and she allowed the confused feelings that the child brought up in her.

Light Of The Soul

Two old friends had very different ways of relaxing. One was a ladies' man and was always on a date, while the other would walk alone though the markets and cafes and observe the habits of strangers.

"Today I saw two old men fishing off the rocks at Bondi beach," the second said. "They had set up fishing lines and were playing backgammon and arguing loudly in Italian, while they waited for the fish to bite... Somehow the oneness of everyone was reflected in their dogged European habits in this Australian setting."

"I saw they same thing in my lover's expression last night," the first responded. "In the moment of orgasm, the same light shines through everyone... the light of the soul of humanity."

Releasing Revenge

Adam felt like someone had broken into his house and ransacked the place, as he stood watching the morning shoppers picking their way gingerly through what remained of the sand sculpture.

“The cleaners must have lost control of the floor polisher overnight,” Zoe said dryly. Some of the sand had been swept away and much of the chalk had disappeared.

"I'm sorry guys," he said. This wasn’t going well, and he felt somehow responsible, which made him want to defend himself. “But I warned you that you were making it harder,” he observed, and then regretted the comment immediately.

"Well, that's it!" Zoe said.

"Don't be stupid!" Sax told her. "We can kick it back into shape pretty quickly."

"Don't call me stupid!" she flashed at him. "There's no point in doing it, if its not being appreciated."

"It's just today," Adam offered in consolation.

"What's the point?" she repeated.

“You didn’t feel like that last night,” Sax reminded her.

“Well I feel like that now!”

Adam’s stomach twisted with frustration. "Just get on with it!" he told her. "I'll talk to the management again, and sort out what happened."

"Fuck you," she responded. "Who do you think you are?"

"What good will talking to the management do now?" Sax supported her and there was a moment of standoff. Adam couldn’t believe that he had allowed himself to get into this position.

“Dad’s right!” Sarah announced, swinging naturally into the confrontation on the side of her father. Her involvement broke the spell however, for she stood with her legs apart, as if ready to draw her gun if necessary, and she looked so fierce that Adam broke into a grin. “You think it’s funny because you’ve got magical powers," Sarah hissed at him, "but Firefly will protect us." She stood tall by her dad, and Adam looked at Sax and grinned.

Sax had a funny expression on his face, like he wanted to laugh but it was too close to the bone, and instead he literally threw himself towards the nearest pile of sand to start work. His foot landed on some loose sand however and he skidded and collapsed onto his backside with one foot doubled underneath him and such a comical look of surprise on his face, that they all burst into laughter.

"Are you okay?" Sarah was full of concern.

"I'm fine," Sax said, "let's just get on with this."

"I'm sorry," Adam told Zoe. "It's just so important what we're doing."

She eyed him warily. "Exactly! Maybe you're taking out some of your own frustrations here!"

"I'm sorry?" he asked, not making any connection to what she might mean.

"Forget it."

"I know it wasn't my place..."

"Forget it Adam!"

He went for a walk and paused outside the door to the management office. He wasn't certain what he was there to achieve, and he felt upset and off balance by all the drama. There was only one way forward however, so he knocked and opened the door. "Is the boss in?" he asked the secretary.

She shook her head. "In a meeting." The office consisted of one room with a number of desks, and there was no other sign of life. The meeting was obviously elsewhere.

“Did the cleaners have a problem last night?” he asked.

She looked at him blankly.

“The sand sculpture was really messed up.”

She twisted her mouth in an awkward way. “I thought it looked a bit funny this morning.” She laughed. “Not that you could really tell the difference.”

It was his turn to look blank.

“I mean, you would tell, but us in the public...” She was trying to make it right, but sensed that it was just getting worse with each word, and stopped.

He nodded, realizing that there was no point in

discussing it further. "Could I use the computer for a moment to make a sign for the sculpture?"

She shrugged. "I guess."

He sat down at a machine, and started typing. He had an idea that if he could give it some context it would be better appreciated by the shoppers, and he threw together a little background on the artists and the history of their success at the Fringe.

“So do you, like... manage these guys?” the secretary asked.

He looked at her and chose nodding as the easiest answer.

“Is there any money in it?”

He shook his head. His eyes were looking at her, but his mind was chewing over Zoe’s remark. Perhaps resentment at his treatment in Auckland was coming out in other ways.

"That’s a shame,” she said. The clock chimed, and her expression brightened. “I'm just going out to get a cake for my coffee break. Will you be okay here by yourself for a few moments?"

He nodded.

"The machine will take any calls," she said, as she closed the door behind her.

He felt an overwhelming urge to say some things and he sensed that this was his opportunity. He exited from the layout program and double clicked on the Internet icon. His fingers drummed on the table as the dial-up connection was loaded, but once on the net, he accessed the Auckland Festival page within moments.

He wasn't certain what he was doing, just checking it out, he told himself, before realizing with a little sense of horror how much satisfaction the thought of revenge engendered in him. He could tell that no one had worked on the site since he left, and his authority code still operated. He cleared everything from the gossip page, and started typing;

'Open Letter to the Auckland City Council.'

'The cultural development of the city is not assisted by the intrusion of political point scoring into the administration of any civic activity...'

Then, in a moment of insight, he saw the folly of his actions, erased his work and closed the connection.

Outside, he discovered the sun was beating fiercely

down, but he had to get out and clear his mind. He found a shady spot in the park across the road from the Center, assumed a cross-legged position, and tried to settle his thoughts, by focusing his attention on his breath. It took forever because of the internal debate in which he was engaged. One part wanted to call erasing the Auckland letter a cop-out and another was supremely satisfied with releasing the desire for revenge.

It was all distracting him from being right where he was however and, knowing this, he slowly released himself from the debate and began to hear the sounds of the world around him.

As his meditation practice deepened, his mind started taking off on flights of fancy where the drama of the moment was enacted in various ways with various members of the team, and he recognized the emotions coming up, and released the thoughts, but it just seemed to keep going today. He began to get frustrated with himself, and annoyed that he had involved himself in these relationships which were pushing these buttons.

Finally he could let go sufficiently to enjoy the peacefulness and observe without sensation the play of the world about him. He saw that everything was just right, and no mater how hard it was, it would never be easier to deal with than right now.

By the time he got back inside, Sarah and the kitten were off on an adventure and both Sax and Zoe had relaxed into the work and were now immersed in their own process. The drama of the morning, it seemed, might never have been.

He taped copies of his new sign to the floor around the sculpture and immediately people pressed around them to understand what was going on. It was the busy time of day, and some stood around joking and talking, which hadn't happened yesterday at all.

The sculpture was looking good, like a surreal landscape of colored fields and weirdly shaped sand-outcrops in amongst the seats and rubbish bins and other paraphernalia of the mall.

"Do you guys want to eat soon?" he asked.

Zoe looked at him for a long time without responding. It felt like her attention was far away and it was just her body that was there in front of him.

"Maybe you could get us some take-away food," Sax suggested. "Sarah's here somewhere, she was just asking about lunch." He stood and looked around, but the girl was no-where in sight. He was resting his weight gently on one foot, and hobbling slightly as he moved.

"Did you hurt yourself?" Adam asked.

"It's nothing," Sax said.

When Sarah returned, Adam took them out to the park to eat, and Sarah sat straight down and buried her face in a hamburger. Sax had lagged behind, and he hobbled up some moments later.

"Have you hurt your foot?" Zoe asked.

He nodded. "I was a bit too eager when I started work." He grinned sheepishly. "I think I twisted something."

He sat down beside her, and she lifted up his trouser leg to reveal a slightly swollen ankle. "The left foot," she observed. "It's a lesson in trusting your creativity."

"Just what I need," he grinned, "good advice." They looked at one another and laughed. "I always physicalize tensions," he explained. He rotated the foot to show it was okay. "It's not too bad."

"And you need to trust...!" she told him.

"Okay!"

They ate in silence for a while. Adam sensed that there was now a feeling of respect between them, which was born of the experience of successfully encountering hurdles together. "What's the plan from here?" he asked.

Zoe shrugged. "Home."

"I mean with the work?"

Sax shrugged. "Who knows? Do you want to organize something for us?"

Adam pursed his lips. The idea had come up a few times, and he found the prospect of their further companionship attractive, despite the emotional ups and downs. "I don't know where I'd sell you."

"You can just magic something," Sarah reminded him. She had a piece of tomato on her cheek.

He grinned at her faith.

"Maybe to art galleries," Zoe suggested. "Like an installation."

Sax nodded. "We could do it on a percentage basis,"

he said. “Twenty percent would be a normal management fee.”

Zoe laughed. “I don't think you'd earn very much out of it," she said.

Adam particularly wanted her forgiveness, because he felt like he has trampled on the closeness which they had developed a couple of nights ago. "That would depend on how successful you guys were," he told her. "I'm on full pay at the moment anyway..."

They grinned.

Sarah's Special Ring

Sarah found a special ring
It was strong as iron
And could do great magic
It made a sound
When she clicked it against things
And protected the wearer
So no harm could come

Then it broke
And terrible things
Were going to happen
The great magic was gone
But the funny thing was
Things just went on
As usual

Firefly

I was half-asleep as dad put me into the back seat of the car, and I cuddled teddy while he hobbled round to get in the front. It was so early that the streetlights were still on, even though it was already light enough to see without them.

"We're going to share the back seat," Adam told me, as he got in beside me, "but the deal is, no magic."

"Why?" I wanted to know. "Do you, like, use it up?" I wasn't happy with getting up this early and, even to me, I sounded grumpy.

He nodded. "I've done enough for a while."

Zoe got into the driver's seat, started the car and we set off. She put on the radio and we relaxed to the beat as we made our way up the hills around the city. It was spread out below us, just waking up, and the sea sat big and dark in the background.

"Where are we going?" I asked.

"Adam's got it under control," dad said over his shoulder.

That was a funny answer, I thought, and I looked at Adam for an explanation.

He winked. "It's a secret."

I grinned. I liked secrets.

It took ages till we found somewhere for breakfast, and I had to nag and nag before Zoe finally stopped at a highway restaurant. The car park was very full, and although we found one spare space, she parked so close to the next car that I couldn't even open my door enough to squeeze out.

"You're so demanding," she told me, opening her door without looking, and there was a bang as it hit the next car.

I giggled.

Dad looked at me. "I want you to keep it together."

I half smothered a few more giggles to keep him happy, while he opened his door and got out. Then she climbed across.

"Come on!" I encouraged Adam, who had been

asleep. "We're having breakfast."

After our food Adam took over the driving and Zoe came into the back with me. I didn't really mind, because this meant that Firefly and Minx could curl up together between us, and it was so sweet to see them resting like this.

She followed my gaze, and smiled. I wasn't certain if she could see Firefly or not. "Are they cuddling?" she asked.

I nodded. She hadn't quite got there, but there was some hope. "You're not too bad," I told her.

"Thanks!"

"I mean, you're okay," I tried to repair any misconception, "for a girlfriend."

"Not a mum?"

I looked at her as if she must be joking, and she nodded.

As the day wore on however, it became very hot again, and the time began to drag by. The only real thing was the car and everything else took on a questionable existence.

“What time is it?” I demanded.

“That’s the tenth time you’ve asked,” dad told me.

I looked at him and was reassured by his hard stare.

I was beginning to feel like I was the only real person on the planet, and that everyone else was simply acting a part for my benefit. The cars whizzing past the other way probably disappeared around the corner when I couldn’t see them any more, I reasoned -- they materialize as I'm about to come into view, play their role in my interactions, and disappear as soon as I am out of sight -- It made total sense.

Then I realized what this would mean as I got bigger, that I would inevitably take my place as the true leader that I really am, but of course I tried not to let the others in the car see that I knew this.

“What time...?” I caught myself before dad could turn.

Zoe wound down the last few centimeters of her window, which made no difference at all to the temperature, as all the other windows were already fully open and the hot wind from the desert was gushing through the car.

“Next time we should get an air-conditioned rental,” Adam said.

Zoe grunted. “That’s the sort of manager I want.”

“There wasn’t any left,” dad protested.

“Managers?”

They laughed.

I started thinking of my friends at school and I recalled the moment where we decided that magic must have been involved in my trip to Auckland, and how important I had felt. Suddenly I couldn't wait to get back and tell them all about the rest of it and I realized how much I missed them.

Maybe staying at home and talking about the festivals was even more way cool than doing them, I thought, and I imagined lying in bed, and I saw my dolls on the pillow beside me, and my drawings on the wall.

"Dad, is all our stuff okay at home?"

He turned to look at me. "Eh?"

"Is the place locked up, at home?"

He nodded. The road burned away beneath us. "Getting tired of our game?" he asked.

I shook my head. "Course not."

I grew tired and dozed for several hours and when I woke up I was stiff and drenched in sweat. Dad was driving and chatting with Zoe in the front seat. Maybe I was still half-asleep, but I thought I had never seen him like this before. He looked different, younger, softer, not the dad I knew, and I felt a pang of fear.

Adam was now asleep in the back with Minx on his lap.

"Where's Firefly?" I asked croakily.

Dad looked at me in the mirror. "Did you have a good sleep?"

"Where's Firefly?" I demanded.

He shrugged. "She looks after herself."

I hated him when he didn't take my concerns seriously. "She needs our help!"

"Of course she does..."

"You'd be happy if we lost her," I accused him.

"How could we lose her?"

"Where is she then?" It was a telling blow, because he could say nothing to that. He just shook his head and turned back to his conversation, but inside I felt something break and I started tapping on the window with a magic rhythm, which would restore my power.

"I told you to get it together," he told me.

"Well, I'm thirsty," I retorted.

"Let's get a drink then," Zoe said, "if it's that simple."

“It’s not,” I told her.

We did stop, and afterwards I went to the toilet and when I finally emerged I found dad and Zoe kissing, right there beside the car in full view of everyone. It was horrible, and Firefly was nowhere in sight to help.

"You take forever!" I told Adam who had also been to the toilet. No-one was safe now.

"You won't be coming with us next time," dad said, extracting himself from her mouth, "if you don't get it together."

I saw a look of worry cross her face at the tone of his voice and I smiled inside, although I didn't let them see that. "Well you can stick your game then!" I told him, and I dropped Minx and marched off.

There was a garden with a stream beside the restaurant, and I took the path by the water. For all I knew we could be snatched by aliens long before 'next time' came around.

In the middle of the garden was a pond, into which the stream ran, down a little set of rapids. The tinkle of the water as it splashed over the stones was refreshing and I squatted down to watch the goldfish.

It was the sort of place that Firefly loved and I half expected to see her resting in the shadows, but I knew inside that she was really gone and it made me feel very lonely.

There were ferns overhanging the bank beside me, and a shaft of sunlight caught the intricate pattern of moisture on the green surface of the leaves. The little white hairs danced in the light, and for a moment I thought she was there but then I realized it was a trick of the light.

The bank behind the leaves was alive with spider's webs, and ants crawled up and down the stalks, from their home in holes in the bank. They were big monsters.

Then Minx came padding up beside me, and nuzzled my lap. I picked him up and hugged him to my face.

Dad squatted down beside me. I looked up at him. I

was crying now. “What’s wrong?” he asked.

“Firefly’s gone,” I told him. Sometimes he was so stupid.

“How come?”

The fact that he had to ask this, was itself the answer, but you couldn’t explain that to a grown-up. I just hugged Minx and rocked back and forth.

I felt his hand on my shoulder, and let him pull me into a cuddle against him. I was crying. I didn’t really know why.

"I do want to come, next time," I admitted, "if the aliens don't get us first."

He smiled and ruffled my hair.

Oasis

Sarah was moody and was sitting beside me in the front, so I could keep an eye on her, as I took my turn at driving. I was enjoying it, even though my left ankle was throbbing, because it felt good to exercise it.

"When will we get there?" she demanded.

"We're almost there," I assured her.

"Where exactly?" Zoe asked.

"Melbourne," I responded and then, catching her eye in the rear-view mirror, I realized that she already knew that.

Her eyes twinkled at me. "But when we get there?" she asked, turning to Adam who was half-asleep beside her in the back. I couldn't see his response, but I guessed there was none, because she poked him, and he jumped so much that I felt the movement in the car.

"There's nothing organized," he grumbled. The

afternoon heat was making everyone tired and scratchy. I adjusted the mirror so I could see him as well.

"Oh." She considered this. "So we're not in a rush to get there?"

"No rush to get anywhere, " he agreed.

He caught my eye in the mirror and winked, and I felt somehow relieved, but I wasn't sure why. His participation had given me a similar sense of freedom as when Sarah and I had first started playing our game, and I figured it was because I no longer had to evaluate the appropriateness of any action and could just allow it to flow.

I saw some signs for a lake-resort up ahead. "Lets find somewhere nice for a siesta?" I suggested.

There was a chorus of agreement, and so a short while later I turned off the highway and followed some signs towards the lake.

The road quickly became narrow and winding, and took some concentration to negotiate with my sore foot. My intuition about that suburban work in Adelaide had been correct, but I hadn't listened to it because of fear of what might happen to my relationship with Zoe if we didn't keep working. I looked at her in the mirror. Although it had been hard work, we had pulled it off. I changed down a gear to pass a truck, and the stab of pain from my left foot as I applied the clutch, reminded me of the cost of that determination.

"I've got to listen to my intuition more," I told myself aloud.

"You said it," Zoe agreed.

I caught her eye in the mirror. "You don't miss a beat, do you?" The bond between us had actually been strengthened through the shopping center struggle, I realized.

"It's the interpretation that's difficult," she said. "We say we don't listen to it, but often we're just misinterpreting."

"You guys are weird!" Sarah told us.

Adam grunted.

I glanced at Sarah, and she caught my eye and waited for my reaction, but I simply turned my attention back to the road, satisfied that she was okay.

"I need a drink," she said. It sounded like something she was saying simply to fill the hole in the conversation, so I nodded absently.

Minx leapt about on the grass when we got to the lake, his playfulness expressing our collective joy at being released from the confines of the vehicle. He spied a feather floating in the air, stalked it, and leapt repeatedly after it, his young body thrilling to the experience each time, but never quite reaching it's goal.

We all laughed, and even Sarah dropped her sullen mood and joined in.

"They're sooo lovely when they're that age." Zoe giggled. She scooped him up, and he hung like a ball of fluff in her hand, as she ruffled him behind the ears.

"How long are we here for?" Sarah asked.

I shrugged and looked at Adam.

"An hour or so?" he suggested.

Sarah suddenly looked exasperated. "What are we going to do here for an hour?"

"Relax," I told her, "like we said."

"With something to drink," she shouted, like I was a moron, and I realized she must have imagined another café.

"Well, you should have said that," I told her, in a

similar tone of voice, before I could stop myself.

“I did!” she said and we looked at one another. It felt like one of those moments where she was determined to have a problem, and I knew there was no response I could make that would avoid that, so I made none. As a result, the moment seemed to hang in time.

Minx leaped out of Zoe’s hands and bounded between us into the bushes and Sarah threw back her head, in a gesture of defiance, and stalked after him.

I let her go. I didn’t want to, but I had no real choice. I had to learn to get out of her way sometimes, and indeed, I knew at heart, to get out of my own way.

The drama had the effect of scattering the group energy however, which was probably Sarah’s intention, and Zoe and Adam had variously disappeared as if sucked into the open space, or perhaps just thankful to be free of one another.

I locked the car and half-hobbled down to the shore of the lake. It was rocky, and I climbed carefully down the rocks to the water’s edge. I found a smooth rock in the shade of an overhanging tree, and sat and contemplated the world.

From here it looked big and fresh. I could be anywhere on the planet, and I was content just to sit and bathe in the richness of the life about me. A butterfly fluttered past, almost brushing the surface of the water with her wings.

The future gnawed at my attention, but I resisted the temptation to indulge myself. For a long moment I was at peace with the world, experiencing myself as the insignificant flash of life, that we all are, and was satisfied just to be here.

I saw Sarah picking her way along the rocks. She stopped beside some blackberry bushes and picked some of the ripe fruit. She looked both small and helpless, and at the same time full of life and curiosity, as she reached up to extract a juicy ripe berry protected by thorns.

Then something moved in the grass, and for a moment my heart leapt into my throat, until Minx bounded out and I relaxed. The impossible richness and fragility of existence belittled any attempt I could make to control anything, and yet when it came to Sarah it was simply instinct to want to protect her.

The future gnawed at my consciousness again, and again I pushed it away. The need to protect Sarah, together with the impossibility of doing that completely, forced me into a process of trust, and I busied myself with the sensations of the moment.

Soon I heard a melody in my imagination, and felt the mouthpiece of the sax on my lips, and I struggled to my feet and went in search of the instrument.

I found Zoe later, curled asleep in the shade, and I lay on the grass beside her. The air had a special stillness around her, as it does about a sleeping animal, and I bathed in this tranquillity. A breath of wind stirred the bushes about us, but we were untouched.

Through the trees, I saw Sarah bouncing up and down by the car doing a performance for Adam and I caught snatches of their conversation. She was keen to get moving, I knew, and when I saw her heading in our direction, I rolled closer to Zoe and brushed her neck with my lips to wake her.

She rolled onto her back and looked up at me. Our contact retained the peaceful togetherness of our bodies, and I was content just to bathe in the richness of our contemplation. Again I felt at peace with the world, in awe of the miracle of each unfolding moment. I bent my head to hers and our lips touched, and we melted into one another through the soft skin contact.

"Adam wants to know who's going to drive the last bit," Sarah said, standing over us.

I heard the voice, but allowed the urgency to drift past with out disturbing the textural communication with Zoe's tongue. Our eye contact had changed suddenly however, like we were looking at one another rather than into one another, and somehow we made an unspoken agreement to continue the physical later, and our lips separated and our bodies rolled apart.

"Do you want to drive?" Sarah asked Zoe like a sweet angel.

Zoe smiled and shook her head. "I might just stay here," she teased her.

"Well dad can drive then," she said, flouncing off without looking at me.

"She probably needs feeding," I decided. "We better get going." Zoe got effortlessly to her feet and stretched, and the movement looked so enjoyable that I copied her.

"Where will I go, when we get to Melbourne?" Zoe tried a different approach with Adam, as she eased the car back onto the road. She had elected to drive in the end.

“Well...” Adam said from the back, and there was a long pause. Sitting in the front beside Zoe, I couldn’t tell if he was just savoring the uncertainty, and I suddenly wondered if perhaps he really had no plan.

"Just trust him," I advised her.

“Just... trust?” her different emphasis in the echo of the phrase, showed the enormity of the request.

I turned and found him grinning.

“Come on Sax, tell him that we should know," Zoe persisted.

"I like leaving it up to him," I confessed.

"You're hopeless!" She clouted me playfully on the shoulder and swerved a little to dramatize the moment.

Sarah squealed. “I want to know too!” she said.

I look at her and she looked really upset. “I thought you liked secrets,” I said, growing suddenly worried.

Minx jumped into her lap, and she fondled his ears. “I dooo...” she said, considering this, and then she buried her face in the kitten's fur. "I do like secrets," she whispered so that only Minx and I could hear, and I felt relieved that she was still playing. I looked at Adam, and my look must have implored his help, for a change came over him.

"There's a Buddhist sand-mandala installation at the National Gallery," he said. "I'd like to go to that."

"Wow!" I said. It seemed to come at such an opportune time, that it took my breath away.

"What's that?" Sarah asked.

"They make a mandala with colored grains of sand," he explained.

She looked wonderingly at him.

"Do you know what a mandala is?" I asked.

She shook her head.

"It's a picture on which you meditate," he explained.

"Do you know what meditation is?" I asked.

She nodded. "It's..." She looked really serious. "You sit with your legs crossed, and you've got your eyes closed..." She stopped and looked at Adam with a grin. "But then you can't see the sand thing." She pointed it out as if revealing to the emperor about his new clothes.

He took a breath to try again. “This sort you do by watching them as they make the picture.”

“With your eyes open?”

He nodded. “Each part of the design carries a spiritual teaching, which you absorb by contemplating it.”

"I'd like to see it," Zoe said. Her tone had completely changed from the earlier bantering.

"Me too," I said.

"It's probably only once in a lifetime that we'd get an opportunity like this," he agreed. “And the simple act of participating in the ceremony assists in maintaining peace and balance in the world."

“How?” Sarah was now full of questions.

He looked at her, then at me for help. “I’m just her father,” I said.

“You'll see,” he advised her.

"So what's a mandala?" she demanded again.

He smiled. "It's a design which leads us to the center," he said, trying a different approach.

"Of what?"

"Ourselves," he said, "and God."

There was quiet in the car for some time. The various personal dramas were forgotten in this contemplation.

We got to the gallery by late afternoon, and miraculously found a parking place nearby. As we got out of the car, Minx leapt about on the sidewalk, reveling once again in the freedom.

"We won't be able to take him into the gallery," I suddenly realized.

"I'm not leaving him in the car." Zoe was adamant.

"We can take turns going in," Sarah suggested.

It was a good practical solution, and Zoe's look of thanks coupled with Sarah's quick helpfulness, made me look anew at their relationship as we walked to the gallery.

We found the mandala on a raised platform, on which two monks were also crouched, working the colored grains of sand into intricate lines and patterns by a painstaking process of encouraging them to run down a grooved stick to the exact place required by the design. It was a work requiring a great deal of concentration, but also a steady hand, which was relaxed into the task at hand.

I found the quiet focus they generated in the midst of this public space amazing, and I saw parallels with my own way of absorbing myself into the work, and was inspired by the devotion, and the peacefulness of the exercise.

It made me think about Adelaide again, and in my mind's eye I saw the festival site from above, in the wider context of the city around it.

"Amazing how good art gives you a flash on yourself," I said to Zoe, who was standing beside me.

She looked at me. She seemed far away, and maybe hadn't even heard my comment.

"I just saw our work in this sort of devotional context," I explained. To me our actions seemed heroic in that context, as if we were taking part in an adventure, which was larger than life.

She nodded, and put her arm around my waist.

I hugged her, and we allowed the togetherness of the moment as we watched the fall of the colored sands.

"Beautiful huh?" she asked.

I nodded. The rhythmic sequence of forms, each

enclosed in the one before, and enclosing the one after, was like a beautiful landscape.

Sarah hopped irreverently up, and grabbed my free hand.

"Where's Minx?" Zoe asked her.

"He's okay."

"Shall I take a turn?" Zoe persisted.

"Don't worry," Sarah insisted in her turn. "How long do they do it?" she asked me.

It felt like her way of distracting and I didn't answer at first, I couldn't really find one, and then I shrugged. "I don't know darling."

Adam was standing behind us. "It takes weeks," he answered.

"How can they stand it?" she asked. "Don't they have more important things to do?"

"It's a ritual," he explained.

"What's that?" she asked.

"It's a way of doing things to give them a bigger meaning," he told her.

I thought that was a pretty good explanation. "Everything we do is meaningless until we see it as a ritual," I offered.

"It's not so important what we do, as how we do it," Zoe added.

Sarah made a face. "You guys are weird."

"Zen monks make simple things like sitting, walking, or drinking tea into rituals," Adam explained, "and by doing that they change these things into teaching devices on their path."

"I was just thinking of our Adelaide stuff a little like that," I said.

He nodded. "There's something there."

Sarah shook her head. "I'll go back out and play with Minx," she said, but she made no move to go.

"I'll leave you guys here too," Adam said. "I'm just going to make a phone call."

"It's about time," Zoe told him. "We'll expect a detailed report when you get back."

He went to touch something on her shirt. "What's that?" he asked, and when she bent her head to check, he brought his finger up to flick the tip of her nose in a teasingly patronizing way.

Her face developed color at the gesture, and I could

feel her restraining herself from pouncing on him.

"Don't you hate that?" Sarah asked, with a perfect tone of innocence, so that we all laughed.

Mama Chimp & the Otter

Mama chimp was worried. She had started caring for a new child and it wasn't growing right.

No matte how hard she tried to teach it to climb trees, it seemed incapable of it, and instead of talking properly, it could only bark. Then, when she took it down to the stream to drink, it dived in, and now she didn't know where it was.

Minx

Adam bought a phone card and called Barbara in Auckland.

"Are you okay?' she asked.

"Sure." He said. "Why?"

"Just haven't heard from you."

He detected care in her voice, which he appreciated. "We've just arrived in Melbourne," he told her, as if that explained something.

"Who's we?"

"I've taken up with the sand sculptors."

"The dad, or the daughter?" She laughed.

"Not like that, and there's another member now, but it's not like that. I'm doing their management."

"How much management is there to do?'

"Not enough at the moment," he admitted, and they both laughed.

"It's all gone pear-shaped here since you left." She told him.

"Thanks."

"No really," she said, "when I sit on the committee and hear the time wasted because they don't know what they're talking about..."

"Ninety percent."

"I realize now how much of it was your vision, " she said. "Let me tell you what happened yesterday..."

"Don't tell me."

"You'll enjoy it."

He really didn't want to know. "Please, spare me." There was a pause. "I'm actually looking for some work for the sculptors, I thought you might have some ideas?"

"Well... I just had the Colville gathering on the phone... It's this weekend... Remember I was telling you about it?"

"Brilliant!" His heart leapt.

"They provide meals and accommodation."

"What about travel?"

There was another pause. "I heard that they are already over their budget," she said, but her tone of voice seemed to suggest that there might be more than one way to look at it. His intuition reached out in search of other opportunities, however nothing came to mind. "We've still got those airfares left in the sponsorship budget," she reminded him.

He remembered the Air New Zealand deal. "And if they're not used soon, they lapse, right?" He knew that was the situation, but they both needed time to asses the implications of their impending decision.

"Yep," she agreed. "Then they're useless."

"So you may as well offer them to a 'like-minded community organization' huh?"

"I think the Festival Charter does charge me to assist community events with resources where possible, doesn't it?"

"Where possible, without financial burden on the council," he added.

"Mmmm... That sounds like it."

"It does, doesn't it?" he agreed. "Well, if they're going to lapse and you've got no other use for them..."

"It's fine by me."

"Could you phone them through to Melbourne, and

we'll get on a plane?"

"Sure. Go to the Air New Zealand counter at the airport, to pick them up." The phone card was running out, and the machine started to beep at them. "Give me a call when you arrive," she said.

"Thanks for this," he told her just before the card expired.

The air conditioning hit him as he re-entered the gallery.

"So?" Zoe challenged him.

"It's all happening," he said, and he had a sense of pleasure in knowing that it really was. "We're on our way to the airport when you guys are ready."

"The airport," Sarah's eyes went wide.

"Where are we going?" Zoe asked.

Adam didn't have an answer immediately, he hadn't really sorted it out himself yet.

"You're not going to keep doing this?" She leant back against Sax, and looked up at him for support.

He put his arms around her waist "What's your problem?" he asked her, reversing the roles.

"I need to know what's happening," she said.

"Why?" Sax responded.

Their voices were playful and so Adam didn't feel the need to release the game by revealing their destination.

"What if we end up in Timbuctoo, with no money to get home?" she asked.

"Then I guess we'll have a nice time in Timbuctoo," Sax answered, kissing her on the back of the neck.

"Dad!" Sarah hissed urgently. "Not here!" Her voice had a hushed urgency, as if he had forgotten where he was.

Zoe looked like she had been about to push away from Sax and reject his accepting attitude, but this stopped her, and she snuggled back against him instead.

When Sarah saw that her comment had had the opposite effect from what she wanted, she poked out her tongue and stalked off.

They ended up waiting in the departure lounge for hours, which was not a pleasant experience at the end of a tiring day.

The first flight was not until just after midnight, and

then there was a problem with the kitten. "I'm afraid we can't take Minx," Adam explained, as gently as he could to Zoe around 10pm. "It's quarantine issues."

"What do you mean?" She looked at him in disbelief.

"Do you know someone who could look after him?" he asked, “while we’re away?”

She shook her head, the nature of the problem slowly dawning on her.

"Well, he can go to the kennels for a couple of days."

"Never," she said. "I just won't go."

"No," Sax protested. "You have to!"

“Actually I’ve had enough of this,” she decided. “You won’t tell us where we’re going, and I can’t take Minx!” She stood up, picked up her bag, and looked about for the kitten.

He was thankfully nowhere to be seen, which gave a moment’s pause for some intervention. Adam wanted to grab her and shake sense into her, but that hadn’t worked last time, and he was happy to see that he had learnt something from that experience.

"Let's see what else we can arrange for Minx," Sax suggested, reaching out and giving her fingers a little rub, "and then we'll make a decision."

She looked at him and bit her lip, and their contact allowed her emotions to stabilize.

Adam looked at Sarah. She was standing, attentive like an animal. He sensed that something was up, but he didn't know her well enough to put his finger on what.

"Is it America?" she asked, noticing his attention.

"I told you, It's a secret," he repeated, and he went to flick the tip of her nose, but she was too quick, and ran away.

Sax and Zoe returned later, arm in arm.

“We've found a ‘Pet-hotel’ at $100 a night,” Sax said.

“Do you think the budget will stretch that far?” Zoe's look was daring him to say that they couldn't afford it.

He shrugged, raised his arms, and let out a breath through his open lips. “That sounds like very good value,” he assured her, “if there was a budget.”

“There's no budget?”

Adam shook his head.

“So we can't afford it?” she challenged him.

"We have to," he told her, in a tone which suggested it was her who was wavering on Minx's proper care.

She grinned. "Even though there's no money?"

He nodded.

She kissed him on the cheek. "Is Sarah with Minx? she asked.

"I haven't seen either of them."

She looked at Sax. "That girl of yours!"

"What about her?" he asked.

"She's so willful."

"I'd call it self assured," he said. "I try and encourage that."

She shook her head. "That's not what I mean."

"What do you mean?"

They looked at one another. It was inexpressible and their expressions somehow agreed on that.

"I'm going to find Sarah," Zoe decided.

"I'll check airport security," Sax offered.

"I'll stay right here," Adam told them, "In case they return."

Zoe came back twenty minutes later in heated argument with Sarah, but no cat in sight. "... It doesn't feel like you're being honest," Zoe told her.

"You're just being mean to me," Sarah shouted back.

"Come on," Adam urged Zoe, "what's Sarah going to do with the cat?"

Sax arrived at that moment with a security guard, and Sarah ran and grabbed hold of her dad's leg and buried her face in his trousers, sobbing. Sax looked bemused, but happy that she was safe.

"What's the matter?" he asked, rubbing his fingers through her hair, but it appeared she was sobbing too uncontrollably to respond. "What happened?" he turned to the adults instead.

"She's being mean to me!" Sarah suddenly stopped sobbing and accused Zoe. It was too theatrical for credibility however, and it just added to Sax's bewilderment. He crouched down so they were the same height and hugged her to his chest. She rested her head on his shoulder. She was safe and that was really all that was important to him.

Zoe started pacing. The guard watched her. "So there's no more problems?" he asked.

“My cat is still missing.” she told him.

He was heavy set with a big beer gut, and a leer in the corner of his mouth. “Your pussy’s missing?” He eyed her crotch. “I’d love to help you find it.”

She gave him the fingers, and he laughed as if this had been the intention.

Sax looked horrified.

“It’s a young kitten,” Adam jumped in to rescue the situation. “We’ve just booked it into the pet hotel, and it has disappeared.”

The guard grinned. “They often do that. I’ll pass the word on.”

Zoe made a face at him as he turned his back.

Adam felt so helpless to influence the outcome of the drama, that he felt himself becoming more and more detached from the emotional turmoil.

The guard returned with a man from management. “If the cat is here, he would be found and looked after,” the man told Zoe in a caring tone.

“If..?” she shouted and burst into tears. She sat down beside Sax and collapsed her head on his shoulder. Then for the next hour she paced around the terminal, convinced that Minx had to be somewhere.

The pall of her emotions billowing like a cloud about her would frighten off any but the most insensitive creature, Adam thought. He found that the more drama there was, the more he retreated into a quieter inward space, and he was surprised and delighted to discover this reaction. Despite the drama, each moment had a beguiling lightness.

Perhaps sensing this equilibrium, Sarah lay with her head on his lap. "It's Auckland isn't it?" she asked in hushed tones. She was half-asleep and a little grumpy, but had bounced back surprisingly well.

"How did you know?"

"I worked it out from the flight time."

He nodded.

"What are we doing there?"

"I told you, It's a secret," he repeated.

"I won't tell anyone."

He shook his head. "Ssshhhh!" he hushed her. He stroked her hair to settle her down. It was their first cuddle, and he enjoyed her warmth and the soft sound of her breath.

He was beginning to enjoy not knowing what to do, and yet doing it anyway, and was trying not to feel satisfied with the Auckland festival paying for their flights in this way. Considering they were still paying him as well, they were being very generous, and the whole thing was obviously a blessing.

Without Comprehension

"Why do we create the same patterns in our life," Adam asked a friend, "even when these are obviously not constructive?"

The friend called him into a room where a woman was reading a book. "My mother has difficulty remembering things from one moment to the next," he explained. The woman finished her book and placed it on the table beside her. Yet immediately her fingers began restlessly searching until they rediscovered it. Then her face brightened and she commenced reading it again. "For years now, she has read the same book," he said. "Why do you think she does that?"

"Because she doesn't remember reading it before," Adam responded.

His friend nodded. "This is why we re-create experiences," he said, "because we lack comprehension of what we are doing."

Letting Go

It was nearing dawn and Zoe was sleeping fitfully in the back of a house-truck, which had picked them up in Auckland. The vehicle seemed to be constructed of scrap wood and demolition windows and doors, and was swaying dangerously from side to side on the narrow winding road.

At one point, she thought that she heard sirens behind them, and later she was sure that she saw a flashing light through the colors of the stained-glass window in the back door. For what seemed like ages she lay in a half-dream state, considering getting up to check it out, without disturbing Sax and Sarah who were asleep on the bed beside her, but without finding the moment to initiate the action.

Finally she slipped to her feet and crept to the back window, and suddenly she felt wide-awake, for there was a cop car following them. Its headlights and siren were off, but its flashing light was on. Then that too went off, and it followed like a shadow, which seemed even more sinister.

Maybe they had seen her, she thought, and she ducked down out of sight. Adam was in the cab with the driver and she could just see their heads through a connecting window above the bed. They were deep in conversation, but she could not hear what they were saying, and there was no way they were going to hear her, over the noise of the old truck. She wondered if they knew about the cops. They must have seen them, but if they had, they were doing a masterly performance of acting normal.

Whatever was happening, it was out of her control, she decided, and she crawled back into bed and snuggled against Sax. She didn't know why, but she was crying a little, and she felt a shudder of release as her body found refuge in his warmth.

Later she felt his lips on her forehead, his tongue brushing away the tears from her cheeks, and she opened her eyes to find his twinkling back at her. She had been dreaming of Minx, and little moments of joy that he had brought her, and a small sob escaped her lips.

“What is it?” he asked.

"I shouldn't have brought him on the tour," she confessed. "I shouldn't really have animals."

“I thought you were having bad dreams."

"I was. I can't look after animals properly," she told him. She looked at Sarah who was asleep beside them, and the responsibility of a child loomed like an impossible task. The girl was curled around her bag, like it was the only familiar thing to hold on to in the changing world, and Zoe felt another sob escape with her breath.

"You can't be responsible for everything," Sax told her. "You have to allow the chaos."

She wrinkled her nose. She knew that Minx would be fine, of course. She just missed him terribly. “I guess you can’t really do anything else, can you?" she agreed.

Her eyes rested on the line of his neck, the little hairs shimmering in the early morning sunlight, as it bounced across the bed with the movements of the truck. It aroused her. She ran her hand over his backside and down his leg. The covers slid off him, and the light danced down his leg to something which flashed on his foot. It was a silver ring on one of the toes of his left foot.

"You've got a ring on your foot!" She said. "I've never noticed." She stretched out her fingers and touched it.

"My left foot," he pointed out. "I bought it at the airport."

She smiled. "How beautiful."

He turned is face towards her, and their lips caressed, and the electricity of the contact spread from the lips throughout their bodies as they made love.

Later the movement of the vehicle came to a stop and Adam put his head in the back door. "There's a tearoom, if anyone's hungry," he said. "Probably the last chance for a couple of hours."

"What's a tearoom?" Zoe asked.

"Something doing greasy chips, instant coffee and sandwiches," Adam told her. "It's the only thing open."

"Lovely," she murmured, but she struggled to her feet anyway with Sax's assistance. Sarah was still miraculously sound asleep, and so they left her there.

The building proved to be a hideous linoleum and formica creation from the seventies, with checked lace curtains, but Zoe found a small garden behind it, which was empty of people and full of life waking to the new day.

She sat at one of the tables and a bird flew down and sat on the edge, pecking at the bare white plastic as if there were food there. She laughed at its charade, and it flew away.

Adam came out with a parcel wrapped in newspaper, and sat opposite her. He placed the parcel in the middle of the table and unwrapped it to reveal a pile of steaming hot chips. He motioned her to eat, but she didn't want any.

"I'll wait for the coffee," she told him.

He nodded and started eating them himself.

It felt awkward between them. "Why were the cops following us?" she asked, more to fill the emptiness, than any real desire to know. She wasn't even certain now if her memory of the police may just have been a dream.

He looked blankly at her. “Cops?” he asked.

She began to feel stupid. “It must have been a dream,” she mumbled. It felt like it was going to take a while to repair their relationship after his lack of support last night, and the memory of Minx brought up her emotions again.

Sax came out with a tray of drinks, put them on the table, and sat behind her with his legs straddling the bench. She leaned back against him, and the familiar contact released the awkwardness she had been feeling.

She picked up the coffee, took a swig, and savored the taste while she cradled the mug in her hands. The sun wasn’t high enough to warm the air, but the crisp morning was alleviated both by the warmth of the mug and of Sax’s body.

The bird returned, and perched overhead on a branch. He chatted to them, while he walked along the branch, as if distracting them, then glided in a perfect curve to hover above them, before swooping on the chip pile, and flying away with several dangling from his beak.

Zoe laughed, more at Adam’s surprise than at the

bird's cheekiness.

When they got back on the road, it started winding around the coast, and the play of the sunlight, as it glinted off the waves slapping against the rocks outside the window, brightened Zoe's thoughts.

She sat propped up on the bed with cushions, with Sarah still asleep beside her and Sax wedged in the open back door, with the saxophone in his lap.

The road ran right beside the water, and it was so narrow that sometimes it seemed certain that they must drop right into the sea, only to turn at the very last moment.

Every now and again, she thought she heard a scratching sound, but she couldn't find from where it was coming. Then Sax started playing his saxophone. The scene was idyllic, the seagulls following behind them, diving and squawking in the notes of the sax, the smell of the land in the air, and yet her thoughts kept returning to Minx and she desperately hoped he was okay. She stroked Sarah's hair with her fingers.

She closed her eyes and let herself go with the growl of the sax, and the notes took her away from the confusion of her feelings, and allowed her just to be.

She found herself in a half-dream space, in which she was imagining herself back in Sydney, browsing the paintings in her exhibition and evaluating the chances of each being sold.

Sax stopped playing, and stretched out on the bed beside her.

"Just thinking of my exhibition," she said, "wondering how it's going?"

"You should call."

She shrugged. The fear of a disappointing answer prevented her from doing that. "There's no need," she reasoned, "I'll find out when we get back."

They rolled towards one another and kissed, and their lips continued the conversation silently for some miles.

Then Sarah stirred and Sax settled her back down with a few strokes of her hair. The girl was exhausted from the night's travel. Her nose twitched in response to something in her dream, and then her breath settled back into a soft regular rhythm.

Sax smiled. Zoe felt strengthened, watching him

daring to love and care for her in all the chaos, and she released the need to give a form to her new feelings.

They were stopped by security guards at the entrance to festival site. They stood at the cab windows talking with Adam, and then peered into the back. A techno-rhythm was beating out through the trees around them.

Zoe's feelings of paranoia from last night came up again, however after conferring on their mobiles, the security finally waved them through, and they bounced along a newly formed gravel road passed several dance areas with different music beats.

Finally the truck stopped, and as the rumble of the engine died, the dance rhythms combined into a sound like a pervading heartbeat.

"We have to walk from here," Adam said, putting his head in the back. Sarah was still miraculously asleep, but Sax and Zoe clambered out.

Immediately below them was the gully that housed the main-stage, and it was a surreal sight -- a sea of people of all colors, embraced by the lush green trees on the hills. Beyond the gully was a beach, with the ocean stretching away, blue and large, and around them on the hillsides there was a sea of tents, spread out in amongst the trees everywhere they could see.

Zoe drank in the event. “This is a wonderful thing you’ve brought us to,” she told Adam.

“Thanks,” he said. “We’ve all done it. I wouldn’t be here without you.”

Easy

Zoe visited a well-known painter in a dream and was amazed by the profusion of work in his studio.

"You seem to have it so easy," she told him.

He smiled. "I just make the space, and creativity flows in to fill the void." She stood, silent, uncomprehending. "I'll show you," he said. He spread out a new sheet of paper on the table, and gathered some tubes of paint, choosing the colors as if on a whim.

"We have made the space for the work," he said, as he chose one of the tubes and a brush, and mixed the color on his pallet. Then he applied it, in several direct unhesitating strokes to the paper. This was repeated with each color in turn, seemingly without effort or thought, until just one color remained.

Zoe liked the ritual nature of this process. "But

how do you decide where to place each color?" she demanded.

"I don't decide. I just place it as the impulse takes me each time." He took the last color, and applied it to several dull areas of the work, with energetic strokes.

"But what if you make a mistake?" she asked.

"There's no such thing," he replied. "Art isn't about being perfect, it's about being different."

"But what if I don't like what I create?" she asked.

"Throw it away!" he advised. "Don't tell anyone." And the simplicity of it made her smile.

Dad's Lesson

I didn't know where I was when I woke up, and there was nobody else in the truck and loud music outside, but I felt wonderful and I could feel a warm patch and a little heartbeat, through the material of my teddy-bag, so I knew that everything was okay. I stretched, picked up the bag, hopped off the bed, and stepped out of the truck.

Dad was sitting a short distance away, with his back against a tree and I went over and sat beside him. I left my bag on, because I wanted to choose the right moment to reveal my triumph.

He smiled. "How's Firefly?" he asked.

I guess he meant it to be nice, but sometimes he was so stupid, it was unbelievable. "She hasn't been around since yesterday," I explained carefully. "We lost her." I let the silence explain his part in this, by not believing me at the time.

"How can you lose an angel?" he asked gently.

I looked away. "We did," I told him. I felt a tear running down my face.

He put his arm around me. "How?"

"By not believing in her!" I told him fiercely. I pulled away, I didn't want him touching my bag.

"Oh!"

"If you don't look after your things," I explained, "they get lost."

He nodded slowly. "Then it's easy, we'll believe in her, and she'll come back."

"As if!"

"Why not?"

"We're not pretending dad," I explained as carefully as I could. This was important. "That's the difference between pretending and believing."

He looked at me for a long time and I wasn't certain if he was really thinking of what I had told him, or not.

"Did you phone the school?" I asked, prodding for a response.

"Not yet."

"See!"

"See what?

"You need to look after things better!"

He nodded slowly again. Then I felt his arm around my shoulders, and this time I let him pull me into a cuddle. "I'll try," he told me. "I'll try and look after things better." He kissed me on the head.

Adam arrived together with a man who had a yellow baseball cap, with the word 'crew' on the side.

"What's crew?" I asked him.

"It means I'm very special," he said.

"I'm very special," I told him coyly.

"You get this special pass instead," he told me, giving me a plastic card with a string. "It's an 'Access all Areas' pass" he explained, with a wink.

"What does that mean?" I asked. It sounded special.

"It gets you in anywhere," he said. "Backstage, everywhere, like magic."

I grinned and put the string round my neck. This was really something. I was getting excited, and found myself hopping from foot to foot. Then I remembered not to bounce my bag.

"There's a great children's stage," he told me. "You should check it out."

I looked at dad. "Can I?"

He nodded. "If you don't get lost."

"As if!"

He shrugged.

"You just follow the signs to the kids stage," the crewman told me.

"Where will you be?" I asked dad.

"At the sand sculpture."

I turned to the crew-man. "The sand pit is by the food stalls," he said, "you just follow the signs."

"Sand sculpture," I corrected him.

"By the food stalls," he repeated, not understanding my correction.

I looked at dad. "See."

He smiled.

As soon as I was out of site of the others, I let Minx out of my bag. He stretched and leapt about, happy to be free. There was a smell from the bag, but that was natural because he wasn't like Firefly, and I found it was mainly on one of my old dresses, so I put it under some ferns to dry out.

"I'm sorry I kept you in the bag all that time," I told him. I held out my hand, and he scampered over to lick my fingers. I held him by the neck and bent forward while I whispered in his ear. "Don't ask any questions, it's for your own protection."

Then I let him go, and he bounded up the path a short distance, then stopped and waited for me to follow. I giggled, and ran after him.

The first thing we found was a large face, which was made like a gate, right over the path so that we had to walk into the mouth and then climb up some stairs in the dark, inside the head.

They had made it like it was the haunted house at a fair, and I carried Minx. I was glad I had him with me, for he was purring so loudly, no mean or nasty thing could get us.

We came out at the top on a tower, which stood like a fort on top of everything. The kids' area was like a fairy-tale landscape.

In front of us was a massive climbing frame, hung in the trees, consisting of ropes and ladders, and poles and swing-bridges.

I put Minx down and he scampered off across the first bridge, and then stopped and waited again. I followed more hesitantly, because the bridge moved with every step I took.

There were lots of other kids playing, and we became part of several gangs, as we competed to negotiate the ropes and poles. Minx was the best of course, and I was pretty special because of him.

We found a mud-slide down the hill beside a stream, and the kids playing on it were all covered in mud. Some were in their underclothes and others were fully clothed, but it was hard to tell under all the mud.

"Some of them are naked," I whispered to Minx, who was watching beside me from one of the swing bridges. You couldn't really tell until they jumped in the stream to wash off. If they didn't wash off straight away the sun dried the mud and it formed a hard skin, which cracked as they moved. "It must feel yucky," I said, but I secretly admired their courage to get dirty like that. This was really living.

Then a loud drum beat started somewhere in front

of us, and we ran along the bridge, climbed down a ladder to the ground, and followed the sound to find a clearing in the trees.

Insect creatures in red suits were dancing out of the trees. They were really people, with poles on their arms and legs, so they looked like spiders, and they were moving towards a stage built out of one part of the climbing frame.

We found a place on the grass in the sun to sit and watch. The drummers sat in front of the stage and the insects acted out a story. It was something about a boss insect, who couldn't do something and the others were helping with different answers.

I lost track of how long I'd been watching, before I lay back and looked up at the clouds and my thoughts drifted.

Suddenly I woke up and I knew dad was waiting. It must have been hours, because the stage was empty and there was just a few kids running around in the clearing. Minx was curled asleep by my nose, so I scooped him up, put him in the bag, and climbed quickly back through the frame.

After a while I started to smell food, and I remembered that the sculpture was beside the food stalls. I also realized that I hadn't eaten for ages and, as I followed the smells, my tummy began to rumble.

I found dad beside what looked like a sand-pit, full of people. I took his hand. "I was getting worried," he said sternly, but his eyes were kind, as he looked down at me.

I nodded. "I know," I told him.

We stood like that for a while.

"What's everyone doing?" I asked.

"They all wanted to take part." He shrugged.

"But it's just a mess," I said. Everyone was doing their own thing with little regard for what anyone else was doing.

"We'll see how it goes," he advised.

I felt Minx moving in my bag, which made me think of Zoe, and at that moment she arrived. I had that power sometimes, and it freaked me out, because I never knew when it would work. She walked up with Adam and another woman.

Adam whistled at something the woman had just

said. “They had a car following us last night,” he explained.

“Following us?” I didn’t know what he meant, and it was hard to hear what he was saying over the beat of the dance music.

“As acting director I had full authority to support it,” the woman said.

“This is Barbara,” Adam introduced her. “The Auckland Festival provided the sponsored airfares to cover our travel here.”

“Who was following us?” dad asked.

“The council,” Barbara said.

“Why?” dad asked.

“To check that you were really doing what I had said you were,” she explained.

“What’s that?” he asked.

“Sand Sculpture at the Colvile Gathering,” she said, gesturing to the sand and, seeing the hive of activity in front of us for the first time, her expression froze for just long enough for it to be funny.

Zoe giggled. “And I thought I was going crazy.”

“You are,” I assured her, and then I bit my lip. We

looked at one another, and I realized that this was the moment to tell her, and that she knew that there was something to say, but I didn't know how to say it, and then I felt stupid, and I just wanted to run away and hide. Feeling this, she put her fingers to her head and made a funny sound as she moved towards me, and I was happy for the game, so I ran away to encourage her, but she stopped and went back to the others.

They were all standing looking at the sand. Some of the people in the sandpit had started to play with sand fights and several couples were burying one another. Adam suggested something, but I couldn't hear what he said because of the music.

"Maybe later," dad replied. "Why don't we let them play?"

Adam nodded.

"We could get something to eat," I suggested hopefully. My tummy was rumbling.

"When did you eat last?" dad asked me.

I found that a hard question to answer. It had been a long time.

There are no Mistakes

Eyes in the Wind

Adam had been leading the way on a trek up the mountain behind the festival site, but then Sarah skipped passed him up the path. The sun was about to go down and the golden tinge to the light on the green leaves was beautiful.

"The colors are so rich at this time of day," Zoe said. She rubbed her hand up my back.

"So beautiful," I agreed. I was blissed out, and enjoying the feel of the wind in my face as we climbed up out of the trees. "Good energy, this gig," Adam said, stopping to wait for us.

"Beautiful," I repeated, pausing beside him, and looking out through the trees over the festival site, which was pumping away below us, a seething mass of people with a pervading beat, which had thankfully grown a little quieter up here.

"Come on you guys!" Sarah called from up ahead. She liked being a strong taskmaster.

The path became steep and narrow a little further on as it wound up a bluff, and my breath started coming in gasps, and my ankle started feeling sore again.

At the ridge the wind had worn a hole right through the sandstone, like a doorway, so that we could clamber through and the path led on beyond.

"Welcome to the magic mountain," Adam said as we each stepped through.

"Magic?" Sarah asked. Her voice was hushed.

He nodded. "You'll see."

The path got more precarious however and soon got to a point where part of it had fallen away completely. We managed to pick our way around it, but by the time we had negotiated a number of these, and then came to one which seemed totally impassable, it began to feel like we were trapped.

Sarah started whimpering, and I held her to reassure her. It felt like something was moving in her teddy-bag, but I didn't have time for it now.

"We're fine," Adam assured her. "Watch me." He

grabbed an overhead root sticking out of the cliff, and swung deftly across the gap. I admired the way he was so unhesitating.

Zoe grinned, and followed him.

The expanse of the sea sat vast, blue and still in the background, putting our moment to moment struggle in a very different perspective.

Sarah stopped crying. "I can't do it," she said. "I'm too scared."

"We'll go back, " I told the others. "You guys go on."

"Sarah!" Adam called, and she lifted her face out of my chest to look at him. "We're on the way to a magical place, so do you really believe we could come to any harm?" She considered this. "Do you really believe we could?" he repeated.

She looked up at me, and I realized that this moment of decision was crucial, if she believed, she would be able to overcome her fear. I smiled, in recognition of our earlier talk. "It's not just my lesson," I told her. "We're all learning it."

This prodded her into action, and without saying anything, she let go of me, grabbed the root and swung across, and I followed.

Above the bluff the bush had been cleared and had reverted to scrub which we had to push through, negotiating the brush of the foliage. The path seemed to twist and turn and we lost it so many times that I was sure there was none.

"You do know where we're going?" Zoe demanded of Adam.

He smiled at her, and for a moment he may have answered either way, but then he nodded. "Of course," he told her.

Finally we stepped out of the trees onto a windswept sandstone outcrop, and at the base of that there was a bank of sand which must have been swept out of the rock itself and collected in a hollow of the outcrop.

We sat on the sand and enjoyed the view. The sand gave way to a smooth rock surface projecting out from the hill, and beyond this was empty space and then the deep blue of sea.

"It's much better than they said," Adam decided.

It was like we were on a beach on top of the world.

The festival was still beating away in the valley beneath us, but up here, the sound was mixed with the cry of birds and the chatter of the wind.

Zoe looked at him. "You bastard, you said you knew where we were going!"

"I did!"

"But you've never been here?"

"You didn't ask that."

She clouted him on the shoulder.

"Come on guys," I told them.

He grinned. "I'm going to meditate," he said, and he moved a little distance away, and crossed his legs.

"It looks like it goes on forever," Sarah said, looking out to sea. The border between the sea and the sky was not clear, and the endless horizon put all our little plans and worries into a different perspective.

"I'll let you into a secret," Adam told us, "It does."

Suddenly I realized what he meant and I wished I could hold on to that moment forever, it was so eternal, and then in the same breath saw how this negated the very insight itself and I smiled at myself.

"For ever?" Sarah's eyes were wide.

He nodded.

We looked at one another.

“And ever?” Zoe asked. Her eyes twinkled in delight at the conversation.

He nodded again. “Best to go gently,” he advised, and his voice had a deep gravelly quality which seemed to travel through all eternity to reach us, before he closed his eyes.

Sitting with the panorama of the horizon behind him, he made a beautiful image, but also one that was a little precarious, as if with one wrong move he might fall into space. There was no movement however, just a deeper and deeper stillness. The world indeed seemed to go on and on from up here.

Sarah put her head in my lap. Her backpack sat beside us, and every now and again it seemed to shake and suddenly I realized that there must be an animal in it.

“Watch out,” I said, and I pulled her away. She grabbed onto me, startled. Zoe also looked at me as if I was weird. "There's something in the bag," I said, but it was doing nothing now.

Sarah started grinning, which seemed a strange reaction, and the bag shook again, and there was a muffled squeaking sound.

Zoe went to investigate, and I felt Sarah stiffen against me. I held her, as Zoe gingerly opened the string at the top of the bag, and then a little fury head popped out, and Minx pounced out of the bag.

Zoe's face lit up and Minx leapt about, mewing joyfully to be free, before she grabbed him and hugged him so hard I was worried for his health.

"I heard you say he would be left behind," Sarah was gabbling her words, in the effort to justify herself. "So I just brought him." She bit her lip, and cuddled against me seeking refuge from the emotion she expected from Zoe.

"Why didn't you tell me?" Zoe asked.

"I thought you'd want me to do it," Sarah said, "but I thought you'd have to stop me if you knew, so I didn't want to tell you until we got off the plane... and since then I haven't known how to tell you..." Her words trailed off.

Zoe looked at me.

I felt like I should tell Sarah off, but didn't quite know what for. It seemed that she had substituted Minx for Firefly, and I although I didn't like the deviousness of her actions, it seemed to be a choice for reality.

"At least Minx's safe," I said, trying not to take sides.

Zoe sat and buried her face in Minx's fur, and he purred loudly.

Adam was still sitting totally still in meditation, like a little Buddha and I noticed a blissful expression on his face.

Suddenly he reminded me of my laughing Buddha at home, and I looked about me with new eyes, and saw that I had created my dream without any conscious intention, and in this I found a new understanding about the power of letting it happen.

I felt happy, picked up my sax, put it to my lips and allowed my feelings out in the notes. They seemed to meld with the birdcalls, the whispering of the wind, the beat from the festival, and Minx's bounding against the sunset, to form a predestined wholeness. In its infinite complexity but unbelievable probability, this was clearly a miracle, and the images, feelings, and sounds danced together and celebrated this experience.

How Books Grow

Books grow in the unconscious, a writer said, and the mind tries to articulate them, with more or less success.

Each stage of the process requires different skills; at the start we need a playful acceptance which allows ideas to be thrown around without any analysis.

Later, lots of rich daily experience, and yet a stable and regular life, to sustain the discipline of the writing practice. Courage to change and yet peace of mind to allow.

Perseverance is required during the re-writes, when honing the unpolished gem is less interesting to the imagination than dreams of its inevitable success.

Then finally, after much fussing and pruning, but never enough, the book just tumbles out of the unconscious almost through sheer exhaustion of bearing the burden.

www.ingramcontent.com/pod-product-compliance
Lightning Source LLC
LaVergne TN
LVHW091025080826
845145LV00002B/359

* 9 7 8 0 9 5 7 8 8 4 4 0 3 *